THE PL

A hawker came to our table with a case displaying a collection of the most exquisite gold rings. I couldn't resist picking one out to examine it and found the ring was fashioned from two halves, joined with a tiny hinge and fastened shut with a concealed catch.

I idly placed it on my little finger and held it up to the light. To my bewilderment, everyone began to laugh.

'That, my little innocent,' said Angel, 'is a pleasure ring. It's meant to be worn on a much more intimate portion of your anatomy!'

And, despite my vehement protests, she insisted on buying it for me as a token of our friendship . . .

Also available from Headline Delta

Lust on the Loose
Lust at Large
Amateur Nights
Amateur Days
Bianca
Compulsion
Two Weeks in May
The Downfall of Danielle
Exposed
Indecent
Fondle in Flagrante
Fondle on Top
Fondle All Over
Hot Pursuit
High Jinks Hall
Lust on the Line
Lust under Licence
Kiss of Death
The Phallus of Osiris
Passion in Paradise
Reluctant Lust
The Wife-Watcher Letters
Amorous Appetites
Hotel D'Amour
Intimate Positions
Ménage à Trois
My Duty, My Desire
Sinderella
The Story of Honey O
Total Abandon
Wild Abandon

The Pleasure Ring

Kitt Gerrard

Copyright © 1997 Kitt Gerrard

The right of Kitt Gerrard to be identified as the Author
of the Work has been asserted by him in accordance with
the Copyright, Designs and Patents Act 1988.

First published in 1997
by HEADLINE BOOK PUBLISHING

A HEADLINE DELTA paperback

10 9 8 7 6 5 4 3 2 1

All rights reserved. No part of this publication may be
reproduced, stored in a retrieval system, or transmitted,
in any form or by any means without the prior written
permission of the publisher, nor be otherwise circulated
in any form of binding or cover other than that in which
it is published and without a similar condition being
imposed on the subsequent purchaser.

All characters in this publication are fictitious
and any resemblance to real persons, living or dead,
is purely coincidental.

ISBN 0 7472 5580 6

Typeset by Palimpsest Book Production Limited,
Polmont, Stirlingshire
Printed and bound in Great Britain by
Cox & Wyman Ltd, Reading, Berkshire

HEADLINE BOOK PUBLISHING
A division of Hodder Headline PLC
338 Euston Road
London NW1 3BH

The Pleasure Ring

Chapter 1

The Kingdom of Pernia, Arabia. 1785

When Ladisa knocks at my door I'm already waiting for her, sitting on the edge of the bed with my robe loosely gathered round me. She enters, smiling in greeting. As she crosses the room to lay down the tray she's carrying, I slit the silk gown open to the floor.

I'm not wearing anything underneath it.

I lean back across the soft mattress, deliberately parting my legs for her. I'm shaved completely bare, razored by her every morning for the past six weeks until, now, my sex is as smooth as polished marble.

She picks up a bottle from the tray and, opening it, pours out a few drops of clear, sharp-smelling liquid into her cupped palm.

Even though I'm bracing myself in anticipation I can't help gasping when she suddenly splashes the stinging lotion all over my fleshy mound.

She quickly presses her hand against me, massaging the liquid in before it trickles away down between my thighs. Her fingertips linger a moment or two longer than necessary, just as they always do. I bite my lip as the familiar burning sensation starts to creep up into my belly.

She selects a second item from the tray: a lightweight,

wooden paddle, its blade long and flat, planed thin to make it as flexible as a whip. She places her free hand on my knee, forcing open my legs wider still as she raises the paddle above her head.

A moment's pause and then the blade makes a sound like wind rushing through trees as it cuts down through the air to land on one verge of my damp sex. I cry out involuntarily. She lifts her arm and smacks me hard with the blade again, this time landing the blow on the opposite slope of me.

The wetness of the lotion makes the strokes sting all the more. I look down to see my pink skin flushing bright crimson, puffing up and thickening already.

I make no effort to stop her, but I thank God that this is the final time I shall have to endure this. At long last, tomorrow is to be the day of my Ordeal by Climax.

My preparations have been long and trying. I've been denied sexual release for the past forty days and every night before sleep I've had to allow her to chastise me like this to increase the sensitivity of my vulva even further.

Of course, we're both aware that there's another reason as well. If the urge to relieve myself should become too great to resist during the night, I will be much too tender to touch myself enough to reach orgasm. I know I can only hope to do well during the Ordeal if I submit myself tightened to breaking point with sexual frustration.

By the time she finishes, my eyes are pricking with tears. Every part of my sex, even my clitoris, is smarting and swollen.

Lifting my legs with sisterly understanding, Ladisa helps me swing round gingerly onto the mattress. She whispers her goodnights and then, pulling a quilted throw over me, leaves me to rest.

The Pleasure Ring

As I lie in the darkness, I let my fingers stray down to my special gold ring, trying to console myself with the thought of how close I am, at last, to gaining my revenge on the evil woman who first gave it to me two long years ago, halfway round the world in Paris.

Little do I realise that, even as I fall asleep, she is hatching one final, desperate plan to cheat me yet again.

Chapter 2

The month after reaching my eighteenth birthday I had been sent to Paris by my parents to stay with my aged aunt. She had many connections in aristocratic society and, although nothing was ever mentioned directly, I knew they all hoped that she would be able to make some glittering match for me; find a suitably rich, young nobleman who would fall in love and propose.

I had only been in the city two days before I was introduced to Angel, the Countess Angelique du Mornay, when we met, I thought quite by chance, at the salon of a certain Madame Valoise.

I was immediately dazzled by Angel's sophistication and style. Although she was only some three years older than I, she was everything I wanted so desperately to be. I know everyone kept telling me how pretty I was but, compared to her, I was just a fresh-faced country girl. She was absolutely beautiful; jet-black hair and flashing hazel eyes.

To my astonishment, she seemed to like me too. I was tremendously flattered when she gave me her calling card as we left. But my aunt was furious. She lectured me sternly that Angel was a dangerous woman, a libertine who was notorious for parading around pretending to be a lady whilst, at the same time, all Paris was alive with the rumours of her promiscuous adventurings. She told me that she feared it was no coincidence that Angel had happened to visit whilst we were at Madame Valoise's. She would have known full well that this was going to be one of my first outings into Paris society and it was plain she had deliberately arranged for our paths to cross.

My aunt practically ordered me not to have any further contact with Angel but, of course, being young, this was almost as good as telling me to do just the opposite. In an act of headstrong defiance, I deliberately set out to go against my aunt's wishes. Although I do see now that really this was less to vex her than to show Angel how spirited I could be.

I met Angel almost every day and, although she was so much more worldly wise than me, I truly believed we had become firm friends. When I repeated to her my aunt's warning, she just laughed and told me that people made up such stories because they were jealous of all the fun she had.

There was no denying, though, that she was shockingly unconventional. Some of the things she did were quite outrageous, but she just didn't seem to care what anybody thought about her.

She was like an older sister to me. She became my confidante. I found I could talk to her about things I'd never spoken of to anyone else. By subtle encouragement she was able to persuade me to tell her all sorts of intimate details about myself.

One day, only a fortnight or so after we'd first met, she told me she thought it was time that I experienced the more 'adult' delights that Paris could offer and that she had decided to appoint herself as my guide and tutor.

It appeared my education was to start immediately for

The Pleasure Ring

that same evening we drove out in her carriage to a country inn hidden away in the forest of Fontainebleau. It was a long way from the city, but on our arrival I was surprised to find the driveway lined on both sides with elegant town carriages.

I had never been in a place like this inn before. Everywhere was in darkness, lit only by the glow of a huge log fire. A gypsy band was playing wild music; men and women were sitting at rough wooden tables, drinking and laughing loudly. But behind all the gaiety there was an undercurrent of tension I couldn't understand.

Angel seemed to know most of the men there. She was stopped numerous times on our way across the room to meet her waiting friends.

After Angel had introduced me and given me wine, I began to look around me. All the dimly lit tables were being waited on by young serving girls. Each wore a loose cotton blouse and long skirt and, it seemed to me, very little else. As the girls brought round the jugs of wine, the men at the tables were quite openly caressing them. I was shocked to see them pushing their hands up the girls' blouses and under their skirts, even so far as to occasionally expose the rounds of their buttocks.

Then I felt Angel reaching over to touch the back of my hand, quietly attracting my attention without alerting the others. She motioned with her eyes over towards the farthest, darkest corner of the room.

In the shadows a man was sitting alone at a table. A serving girl had made her way over to him and was placing a jug of wine in front of him. As she turned to go, the man pushed a silver coin across the table at her. The girl picked the coin up and, quickly checking about the room, pocketed it before sliding round to the other side of the table.

Then, quite clearly, I saw her loosen the man's britches and hitch up her skirts as she sat down on his lap. They started to kiss and I could see the man nuzzling his face down into the girl's blouse.

Although I had never ever seen it being done before I just knew for certain that the girl was letting the man have her. She was actually riding up and down on him now, holding on tightly with her arms round his neck as he thrust up inside her.

I knew it was wrong to go on watching them, but I couldn't tear my eyes away. It is impossible to describe how arousing I found this sight. My head was swimming, my stomach fluttering, my sex felt as if hot syrup had been poured over it. It was the expression on the girl's face, the way she somehow looked hot and worried and in pain all at the same time; the way their bodies moved together furtively.

Then, suddenly, I saw the man begin to buck violently and I knew he was coming. To my great excitement I saw the girl tip her head back and mouth a long but silent 'Ohhh!' as she climaxed with him. Her whole body seemed to go rigid before she collapsed limply over his shoulder, shuddering in pleasure.

My mouth felt very, very dry. I was unable to recover myself properly before Angel caught my eye and smiled at me knowingly.

Further discomfort was only spared me by the timely arrival of a hawker selling his wares. He was holding out a wooden display case studded with a collection of the most exquisite gold rings. They were so unusual I couldn't resist picking one out to examine it. For some curious reason the ring was fashioned from two halves, joined with a tiny hinge on one side and fastened shut with a concealed catch on the other.

I idly placed it on my little finger, the only one it would fit and, snapping it closed, I lifted my hand up to admire it in the firelight.

To my bewilderment everyone began to laugh at me, but it was Angel who finally explained the joke.

'My little innocent, that is a pleasure ring. It's not for your finger. It is meant to be worn on a much more intimate part of your anatomy!'

I couldn't help my face reddening madly when she leant over to whisper in my ear that the ring was made like that so that it could be closed behind the swollen clitoris. It was designed to hold it standing proud of the sex, proffering it out so that the stimulation of lovemaking and the joy of orgasm were greatly increased.

Despite my vehement protests Angel insisted on buying the ring I'd chosen and giving it to me as a token of our friendship. I could not refuse her and I must admit that by this time I was secretly aching with excitement at the idea of experimenting with the ring when I returned home to my aunt's that evening.

I will also confess, now, that ever since I had arrived in Paris I had been indulging in The Maiden's Vice quite shamelessly. At home in Angers I have to share my room with my two younger sisters and there has never been any opportunity for me to touch myself at night in bed. I have always had to go out of the house during the daytime to find some quiet barn or wooded copse on the estate and relieve myself there.

However, since I've had my own room at my aunt's, I've been free to masturbate myself without restraint and, for the first time, I have discovered the pleasures of the candle. (Though I have been very careful to remember the old wives' tale that you can always tell when a young girl has fallen into The Vice by the way there is always one of her candles that never burns down as far as the others.)

Not that I haven't had my scares as well. The first night I brought myself off like that I loved it so much I did it again and again until I eventually fell asleep, exhausted with coming. I must have lain on top of the bed all night long, stark-naked with the candle still clutched in my hand. When the maid came in the next morning, I only had the briefest moment to cover myself up. Even now, I'm not completely sure she didn't catch a glimpse of the round-tipped wax shaft before I managed to pull the sheets over myself.

This night, though, the candles would stay in their stand. I undressed quickly and stood in front of the mirror. I unwrapped the ring and pulled it open with trembling fingers. There was no need to prepare my clitoris. It was already hugely stiff.

Watching my reflection, I parted my legs and pressed the ring back behind my tender nub. With a jerking groan, I snapped it shut. My clitoris was left captured, gathered together and displayed out from between my lips like a tight, round, cushion button.

I knew straight away I'd been given something wonderful. Cautiously, I took a step forward. The moment I moved I almost doubled up as the bouquet of sensuous flesh grazed against my labia and sent out a shock of pleasure that went right through me. I steeled myself and took another step. Then another.

I tried to walk across the room but only managed five or six stiff-legged paces before the stimulation was too

The Pleasure Ring

much. I could feel my knees going weak. I reached to lean against the chair standing at the end of my bed, but even the movement of steadying myself just caused more unbearable sensation. I felt myself losing control, felt the start of orgasm pulsing out from inside the ring, spiralling away, spilling out of me.

I collapsed into the chair, wrung out with the ecstasy of violent climax, just like the serving girl I'd watched at the inn. And all the time I was coming I had to squeeze my sex lips together as tight as I could, had to hold the ring completely still because it was impossible to bear even the slightest stimulation whilst I was coming off.

It was the first time I'd ever reached climax without touching myself. The ring had forced my body to have a 'self-inflicted' orgasm. And it was so different, so much more intense than any I'd known before, that it made all the others seem like girlish play.

Somehow, I felt the ring had given me my first real 'woman's' orgasm.

Chapter 3

Now, a week later, I'm sitting in the back of a cab, clattering through the darkened, cobbled streets of Montmartre. I'm full of anticipation. Angel is taking me to visit the opera for the very first time. I'm dressed in the expensive new outfit that she helped me choose especially for this evening. It's the latest fashion – a full, hooped skirt of silk, worn with a tightly corseted matching jacket. Angel and all her friends are wearing them at the moment.

They're all a little older than me and their bodies are much fuller than mine. At first I thought my figure was still too undeveloped to carry off such a style, but Angel wouldn't hear of it. She absolutely insisted that I chose this design for tonight.

My carriage arrives at the steps of the opera house. As uniformed attendants step forward to help me out, Angel comes down the stone steps to greet me. She takes my arm and escorts me into the foyer. I see heads turning all around us, people whispering disapprovingly. We seem to create quite a stir – it's a heady feeling to be the centre of so much attention.

Angel ignores them all completely. She leads me through a doorway and we climb a long, narrow, candlelit stairway up to a dark corridor that has a row of doorways opening off down the side of it. Angel stops at one of them and ushers me through into her reserved box.

My first sight of the theatre below is even more wonderful than I imagined. We're high up at one side of the upper circle, looking right down across all the hundreds of richly dressed people sitting in the seats below us. There are chandeliers burning, the brightly coloured stage, the noise of the orchestra tuning up, the babble of excited conversation.

The box itself is like a very small room but with the front area of the carpeted floor stepped down a foot or so. Two rows of wooden chairs are arranged facing the stage, one on the lower front level and one directly behind on the higher level. There are heavy curtains at the back of the room that can be drawn to keep out draughts. We're separated from our neighbours by high side walls that come so far forward no one would be able to see in from the next boxes even if they leant right over the edge of the balcony. It's totally private.

Angel's other guests have already arrived. There are six of them, all women. I notice straight away that every one of them, including Angel, is wearing the same sort of dress and jacket style that she chose for me.

I can't help feeling it's a little strange that they've all remained standing whilst they've been waiting for us. They were all talking as I entered, but the moment they saw me they fell silent. For a few brief seconds I have the uncomfortable feeling that their eyes are somehow searching over my body. But then they catch Angel's angry glance and hastily avert them.

I don't understand what's going on and there's no time for me to think about it because, just then, the lights in the theatre are dimmed to warn us that the performance

The Pleasure Ring

is about to begin. I nod my greetings to them hastily and move to take the chair on the front row of seats that Angel indicates for me.

I immediately see a problem. The box wasn't designed to accommodate so many women wearing such full evening skirts. The hoops will take up so much space there isn't going to be enough room for everyone to sit down.

When I mention this to Angel, she just laughs conspiratorially and tells me there's a simple answer. Going to the door, she turns the key in the lock before pulling one of the draught curtains across and disappearing behind it. When she emerges again I'm staggered to see she's removed her skirt and has it in her hand. She drops it to the floor at the back of the box and brazenly takes her seat wearing only her jacket and leg stockings.

Taking her lead, the others do the same, one after another until it only remains for me to follow. I feel very nervous. I've never done such a thing before but, as Angel quite rightly says, no one can see us below our waists, so nobody will ever realise what we've done.

I do it. Slipping behind the curtain, I wriggle out of my skirt and add it to the pile of others.

Feeling very conspicuous, I hurry to my seat as quickly as I can.

The lights go up on the stage and the performance gets under way. It's marvellous. I love everything about it; the music, the singing, the beautiful costumes.

Angel is sitting right beside me. I look towards her, thinking how beautiful she is too. I can't help my gaze straying down to her lap, to the smooth whiteness of thigh that's showing over her stocking tops. Like all the rest of us she's wearing a *bande*, a long, oblong strip of linen passed between the legs and buttoned to the front and back of the undercorset so as to modestly cover the sex. Sitting down has made Angel's gape slightly open at the sides. I find it impossible to resist stealing a glimpse at the dark, matted hair that's revealed below.

But how crimson my cheeks burn when she turns unexpectedly and catches me staring at her like that! It somehow makes it even worse that her only reaction is to smile with amusement. She makes absolutely no effort to cover herself. In fact, I almost swear she deliberately moves in her chair so as to make the gap under the *bande* open even wider. But I control my desire to look again and for a while I'm able to lose myself in the music, concentrate all my attention on what's happening on the stage.

As the performance goes on, though, I start to be distracted by a rhythmic beating noise coming from behind me. I try to ignore it at first, but it keeps getting louder and louder and now there are other sounds as well; material rustling, a chair creaking, faint sighs and groans.

Eventually I just have to turn round. The box is in almost total darkness, but what I'm able to make out just makes me gasp in horror.

The woman directly behind me is sitting with her *bande* unbuttoned, sprawled in her chair with her legs wide open. Her jacket and corset are undone and the woman on her left is kissing and fondling her uncovered breasts. At the same time, the woman to her right is leaning across and toying with the dusky folds of her moist sex. It's very obvious that the woman is near to coming. Her eyes are shut and she's moaning continually.

As I watch, the one kissing her breasts brings her hand down between the woman's legs as well. She's holding a smooth ivory stick shaped like a long, thin, tapered finger. She inserts it into the woman's vulva and starts

The Pleasure Ring

frigging her with it so intensely that it brings her off almost instantly.

The woman orgasms noisily, just a few inches away from me.

I see now that all the other women behind me have these sticks. One by one they release their *bandes* and start to use the things on themselves. I swivel round to Angel in shocked amazement, only to find she too has one of them in her hand.

She hands a small package to me. 'Don't look so scandalised, Amande! We always do this during the opera. It's so very exciting, coming together hidden in the darkness, especially sitting in the front here where there's always the danger of someone finding you out! I've bought this for you. You don't want to be the odd one out now, do you?'

I try very hard to hide my embarrassment, desperately wanting to show Angel that I can be as wild and adventurous as she is. I take the present and unwrap it. The fingerstick inside is made of the palest ivory, the end of it is mounted into a chased silver handle. When I hold it up to the light I see there is a provocative scene worked into the precious metal. It shows a bare-thighed young shepherdess languishing back under an oak tree. She neglects her flock whilst she pleasures herself slackly with a fingerstick instead, completely unaware that a farmboy is hiding in the branches above, masturbating delightedly as he spies on her.

It is a beautiful thing. Shyly turning back to thank Angel, I discover that whilst I was looking away she has unfastened her *bande* as well. I see her quite openly now. Her sex is much more prominent than mine, more rounded and full. She relaxes back into her chair and slides her fingerstick in easily. I want to do the same, but I feel so very inhibited. When I start to undo my *bande*, my nervous hands are shaking too much to manage it.

Angel notices how I'm holding back. She leans over and whispers, 'Perhaps this first time it would be easier if some of the others helped you?'

Before I have time to answer, she motions with her head and, almost as if it were an arranged signal, the women behind me take my arm and draw me out of my seat to join them. I stand up, thinking they're going to make me sit with them on the second row of seats. But they have very different plans for me!

They take me through to the space behind the chairs and lay me down onto the carpet. Two of the women stay with Angel to fill the front row of the box and keep out prying eyes. All the others gather round me on the floor.

They set to work enthusiastically, hands sliding all over my body. Nimble fingers unbutton my *bande* and flourish it away. Out of the corner of my eye I notice one of the women gathering up the damp scrap of cloth and surreptitiously tucking it away in the narrow valley of her cleavage as a keepsake.

My jacket and stockings are removed and then my undercorset loosened. They unlace it and spread it apart, leaving my breasts revealed and displayed like some common whore's. It's so hard to do anything to resist them. I know it's wrong, but it's what Angel wants me to do and it's very, very exciting.

Hands push between my knees, wanting to part my legs. I try to stop them, shamed that when I let them do it they'll all see how wet I've become.

They won't be denied, though. I'm forced apart and the woman I'd first seen being climaxed pushes herself between my legs to keep them spread open. She starts massaging my sex, preparing it to receive my new fingerstick. Whilst the others kiss and stroke my legs and breasts, she works me up with skilful stroking until I'm so ready I hand the ivory rod to her with undisguised eagerness.

She places the tip of it against my lips and very gradually starts probing it into me. She dips it in and out, sinking it in deeper and deeper each time until I'm taking the whole length of it. When she sees how easily it slides in she looks at me and smiles. 'You *have* been touching yourself a lot recently, haven't you, Amande? Trying out your new pleasure ring, no doubt!'

Even though it's true that since Angel gave me the ring I've barely done anything else at night, I feel totally flustered that my secret pleasuring should be such common knowledge.

I turn away from her, too tongue-tied to deny her taunts, and my silence is a total admission of guilt. She quickly sentences me for my sins. 'In that case, I think maybe we'll have to make things a little harder for you!'

She nods to the others and, as one, I feel their hands tightening round my arms and legs. Again it's just as if it's all been planned out beforehand. I look down to see the woman pick up her own fingerstick. She lays it beside mine and then, grasping the two shafts together, she slowly pushes them both into me as one. She stretches me right open, making me catch my breath.

She smiles again and begins to work the twin sticks into me strongly. I can barely take the sensation of them entering me. I try to reach down and stop her, try to struggle free, but I'm not strong enough. I'm at their mercy.

She starts going faster and faster. I'm writhing around now. My hips are the only part of my body I can move, so I buck up and down fiercely. I call out and a hand is instantly pressed over my mouth.

I look over to Angel for help, but she's facing away from me, watching the opera. I feel a surge of hope that somehow she's not yet aware of what's being done to me. I pray she'll turn round and she'll notice and rescue me. But then I see how her hand is working between her thighs, how tensely she's thrusting her fingerstick into her own sex, and I just know it's hearing me being abused so vigorously that's exciting her.

And somehow the thought of her sitting there, listening to me being made to come, triggers my arousal. There's going to be no escape, I'm going to be held down here against my will and forced to orgasm.

The woman's fingertips have found my clitoris. I'm slippery with my own juices. The hand across my mouth is only stifling my panting moans now. I'm suddenly aware that my hips are bucking up to meet the thrusts of the shafts. Then riding on it. Then jerking.

I'm there. The women are doing to me what they wanted all along. They're making me climax so fiercely they have to restrain me like a wild animal as I thrash around on the floor, flailing to and fro as the savage convulsions rack my body. They grip me tightly whilst the coming possesses me and then leaves me broken and tamed.

To my surprise, though, I find that even when it passes their hands stay on me, keeping me held down. For a few moments, I think it's because they want to bring me off a second time and, only half reluctantly, I begin to prepare myself to be taken over the edge again. It's then that I get a terrible shock.

A movement at the back of the box makes me turn my head. A hand is pulling the undisturbed draught curtain

The Pleasure Ring

to one side! As I peer into the blackness the shadowy figure of a young man in evening dress unveils himself from behind it.

With total humiliation, I realise that this man has been observing everything that's gone on. He's seen me being stripped and spread apart without protest, seen me willingly allow my sex to be exposed, seen me masturbated until I've orgasmed in the most lewd way. I can't meet his gaze, I feel so ashamed I have to shut my eyes tight.

It's when I feel the women between my legs moving away that the true nature of my fate dawns on me. The man comes to kneel in her place, his britches pulled down. His member is standing out, swollen and red. He's so very erect and excited it's obvious he's been rubbing himself whilst spying on me from behind the curtain.

The hand tightens on my mouth. My legs are pulled even wider apart. He bends forward and feeds his shaft into me. In all the thousand times I've thought about what my first time with a man would be like, I never once imagined it would be like this.

He feels like the fingersticks, only warmer and softer. He starts to take me with short stabbing strokes and as he leans forward over me he puts his mouth to my ear. 'How are you ever going to explain how you came to lose your virginity like this? How will you explain away how you were entered so easily, why you were lying on the floor in a public place, half naked and already pleasured by another woman when it happened? What *will* people think of you?'

Knowing the truth of what he's saying, I turn to Angel again, eyes almost blinded by tears. The woman I thought of as my friend is standing over me now, playing with herself idly whilst she watches me being taken. She sees me looking at her and her mouth twists up at the corners.

The man starts thrusting into me, pumping himself into my pouting sex, growing bigger and harder all the time.

He's urgent to spend himself inside me but, at the very last moment, Angel calls to him sharply. With the utmost reluctance, he obeys her command and jerks himself out of me. He grasps his throbbing shaft in both hands and arches back, straining. The eye of his shiny, purple head ruptures open and his seed starts to spurt out like water from a hose. The hot, creamy liquid splatters all across my loosened corsets, splashing up onto my exposed breasts and face in sticky, thick droplets.

And as he comes over me I see Angel bring herself off. She falls back against the wall, unsteady on her legs as the climax courses through her. She throws her head back and laughs, cruelly revelling in my torment, despising me for being so foolish and naive as to fall into the trap she'd laid for me.

Chapter 4

I run out of the theatre half undressed, clasping my bodice together over my breasts, still pulling up my skirt. In tears, I give a cab driver directions to take me home.

I go straight to my room and lock myself in.

In the morning I refuse to come out. At first, I won't tell my aunt the reason, but by mid-morning it's not necessary anyway. By then she, and everyone else in Paris, has heard the story of the trick that Angel played on me and the way she'd had me deflowered so humiliatingly.

At midday a maid knocks on my door and informs me timidly that my aunt 'requests' my presence for lunch downstairs. It is obvious from her tone that this is really nothing less than an order.

When I go down to join her there is an icy chill in the room. We sit in silence. I hardly manage more than a few mouthfuls of food.

At length my aunt says simply, 'Amande, you look pale and unwell. It is plain that our Paris air is not suiting you. I think it would be much better for your health if you returned to the country. Immediately.'

There is no doubting her message. By that evening I am packed and on the stagecoach back to Angers.

My aunt sends a letter with me, telling my parents all they need to know of the affair. They move quickly, knowing their only hope of marrying me off now lies in finding someone to take me before news of the scandal arrives from Paris.

Within two weeks I am betrothed to one Charles Sancerre, a local estate owner who is enticed into asking for my hand solely by the generous dowry of land my father offers him. He is a plain, country gentleman, well over twice my age. He seems much happier with his guns and horses than with me and even by our wedding day I have not spent more than a few minutes alone with him.

On our honeymoon night I move into the bedroom that has been readied for me at his manor house. I retire early as is required by tradition and dutifully arrange myself in bed, nervously anticipating my new husband's arrival.

I wait. And wait. And wait.

But he does not come to me that night or any other night. Although the rules of etiquette mean that the subject can never be discussed, I soon realise that, sadly, Charles has no interest in me as a woman nor as a companion. He wants me only as his housekeeper and as the hostess for the almost endless round of dinners he seems to provide for his hunting and riding friends.

It is only a matter of time before I turn to the pleasure ring again to comfort me during the long nights. Even though it was the hated Angel that had given it to me, I hadn't been able to bear parting with the marvellous device when I left Paris. It seems so cruel that, just when I had been gifted with the secret of reaching such heights of sexual ecstasy, I should be denied a partner to share them with. The only stimulation I get now is from the erotic novellas I secretly steal from the maids to read whilst I excite myself.

There is one especially that I go back to again and again, called *Carlotta's Ball*. It is set in Venice and I like it so much

The Pleasure Ring

because the woman in the story, Carlotta, is in the same unhappy situation as I am – married to a man who doesn't desire her sexually. Her husband, Mario, is an ambitious young judge. He seems to care only about furthering his position in society and everything he does is decided by how it looks to others.

On his insistence, because it is the 'proper' arrangement for respectable couples, he forces her to sleep in a separate room. Right from the start of their marriage, Mario has made it clear that Carlotta would only be expected to welcome him into her bed on certain pre-arranged nights and then only for as long as was necessary for him to fulfil his duties as a future father.

He lets her know quite plainly that, as his wife, she must allow these visits but, as a lady, it would be most unseemly if she was ever to give the impression that she either encouraged them or took any pleasure from them.

Whenever he comes to her he expects to find her lying facing away from him. The room has to be in total darkness before he will enter the bed and turn her over onto her back. Lifting her nightdress just high enough to expose her sex, he pulls up his own long gown and then penetrates her, thrusting into her stiffly in silence until he reaches climax. As soon as she feels him spill inside her, he apologises and leaves immediately.

She, though, like me, is a deeply sensual woman. Her need to relieve her sexual frustration makes her resort to The Vice just as often as it has forced me to.

Carlotta is luckier though, for she makes an incredible discovery that changes everything . . .

One day I needed to go into Mario's study to find a bill that required payment. Mario doesn't like me entering his private room and interfering with his papers, but I needed to locate the bill straight away. When I couldn't find it on his desktop I had to begin searching for it in the drawers below.

To my surprise, when I opened the very bottom drawer I came across a small bundle wrapped in one of his handkerchiefs. Curious, I unfolded the cloth to find it held a black leather tube, about four inches long. The inside of the thing was lined with fine suede, but the outside had been stitched so that it was ringed by coarse seams all down its length. At one end a flap of rough fur had been sewn standing out from the top of the tube and on each side below that a short cord thong had been attached.

I was examining this strange object when Mario came into the study unexpectedly. When he saw what I was holding he turned as white as a sheet and, before I could say anything, he snatched it from me. He seemed consumed with embarrassment. He began to stammer out, red-faced, an explanation that the tube was in his desk because it was evidence from a case he had been judging.

When I pressed him about it, he reluctantly told me that a man had been caught with a prostitute, copulating in a graveyard. Normally they would not have been discovered but the woman had been making so much noise that the nightguard had been called out.

It seemed that, when the man was arrested, this disgusting device had been found tied over his member. Mario told me he had been so shocked by this vile sexual attachment that he hadn't wanted anyone else to gain possession of it. He had taken it on himself to bring it home so that he could dispose of it personally.

Saying this he took hold of the tube in his fingers as

The Pleasure Ring

though it could infect him and, striding into the next room, I heard him throw it onto the fire.

I had to go to my room immediately. I kept imagining in my mind what it would have been like if it had been me there in the graveyard with that man wearing the thing slid over his cock, tied round his testicles so that only the purple head of his own shaft bulged out the end of it. Just the thought of having the harsh coldness of that stiff leather sleeve pushed inside me made me feel sick inside. But how it excited me too! I could see now how he would wear it so that the flap of fur grazed against my clitoris every time the hard, ridged tube went into me. I couldn't contain my arousal. I pulled my skirts down and masturbated to orgasm, just standing there in the middle of the room with my petticoats round my ankles.

Soon after that day I came to the decision that, even just for one time, I had to experience for myself the ecstasy of torrid, passionate lovemaking. I had to find out what it really felt like to be driven to orgasm by the abandoned thrusting of a man filled with lust for me.

And, despite all the risks, I knew a way it could be achieved!

Once a year the whole of Venice comes to a standstill for three days. It's a holiday in celebration of our saints and, on the final night of the festivities, grand masked balls are held throughout the city. Every year Mario and I attend the ball at the palazzo of the mayor of Venice.

It's a huge event and every noteworthy civil servant, lawyer and judge is invited. It's a very important occasion for Mario to attend but, despite the lavish hospitality of the mayor, it is always a deadly dull affair.

To add a little extra excitement, Mario and I always keep our masquerade costumes a secret from each other.

We travel to the ball separately and try to identify each other in the crowd. Some years we had been successful, others not. Whether or not we find each other, at the end of the ball Mario always goes on to one of the senior judge's houses for more drinking and I come home alone. So it can often come about that we never knowingly meet during the whole evening.

This year's ball was only a week away, just enough time to lay my plans. I could hardly wait for it to arrive.

On the night I go to my room and dress for the evening. I wait there until I hear Mario departing. As he leaves, he calls up to wish me luck in finding him. Five minutes later, I go out after him, swathed in a full-length, black-hooded cloak.

I make my way across the city through the brightly lit streets. Everywhere there is music playing, people laughing and dancing. Everyone is dressed for the masquerades.

I hurry along trying not to draw attention to myself. Blending into the shadows, I turn off sharply into a narrow entry and cross a quiet backwater canal by a little-used bridge. I glance behind me nervously as I enter a part of Venice that is seldom visited by any true lady.

Already I'm committed, if Mario were to find I'd been here it would be hard to explain myself. The truth is I'm not going to the Mayor's ball at all. Tonight, I'm going to an altogether different type of celebration – tonight, I'm going to secretly attend the erotic Masquerade d'Aphrodite.

Every one in Venice has heard stories about this ball and the disgraceful things that go on there. The Masquerade is so scandalous it's only allowed to take place in an old warehouse well away from the grand palazzos.

I'm nearly there now. My heart is beating so hard I can

The Pleasure Ring

scarcely breathe. I pull my mask into place. It is the rule that every woman at the ball wears the same design, the golden face of Aphrodite, highlighted with rouged cheeks as though she were in the flush of sexual arousal.

Under my cloak I also have on the required costume – a plain toga of gauze muslin, almost totally transparent. It's tied at the waist with a tiny purse on a cord. I'm not allowed to wear anything else underneath it.

I reach the doors of the warehouse. There's no time for second thoughts. The anonymity of my mask helps me shed my inhibitions. Walking straight into the entrance, a servant takes my cloak and, moments later, I'm standing inside the main hall, naked except for my scant wisp of muslin.

I feel as though I've stepped into some vision of Hell. The very air is heavy with lust and depravity. There are torch flares burning in sconces down both sides of the room, casting flickering shadows over a milling throng of people. All the women present in the hall are displaying themselves in the same provocative way as I am. It makes me tremble to realise how blatantly my own body is being displayed. Everywhere I look there are the curving contours of hard-nippled breasts, the rounded globes of pouting buttocks, the dark triangles of half-revealed quims. I know many of the young women here are prostitutes, but I can't help wondering how many of the others are like me, respectable ladies musking like she-cats for the thrill of illicit liaisons.

All the men are in disguise too, but their costumes are even more disturbing, revelling in the darker side of sexual desire. Many have come as horned-masked devils, others as leering satyrs and prowling wolves.

I must wait for one of them to approach me; the rules must be obeyed. In order to protect our true identities, we women are forbidden to speak. We must remain silent at all times and communicate only by nodding or shaking our heads. It is also decreed that the men must pay for everything.

A group of musicians starts up a wild, whirling tune. A man dressed as a demon forces a cup of strong wine on me in exchange for a dance. As we move together he starts to touch me, running his hands over my shoulders and hips. I don't try to stop him.

When the next tune begins I drink and dance with another partner, then another and another. But all the time I'm with them I'm aware that another man is watching me from a shadowy corner of the hall. His eyes never leave me, I feel them burning into my back even when I deliberately turn away from him.

He's dressed all in black. His mask, his jacket, his high boots, even his loose trousers all made of leather. He looks strong and powerful. Under his clothes I know his body will be hard and muscular. He's the one I want.

Made bold by the wine, I drift over to stand in front of him, swaying sensuously to the beat of the music. He doesn't need any more encouragement.

Seconds later we're dancing close together. He holds me tight to him so that my breasts rasp against the strapping of his jacket. All the others had just touched me lightly, but there is no mistaking this man's intentions.

His hands are everywhere on me, caressing and exploring with savage want, even lifting my toga up at the back and fondling my bare buttocks in full view of everyone.

I have no way of hiding my arousal from him. My nipples are standing out like olives and I can feel the growing wetness of my quim. He senses it as well and,

The Pleasure Ring

pulling away from me, he looks down between my legs. I follow his gaze. Behind my mask, I blush crimson to see the muslin all round my belly is clinging to the folds of my mound, soaked through with my own juices. I'm sure he must be able to feel my clitoris throbbing with desire when he reaches forward and slowly tugs the cloth free.

Looking into my eyes, he takes a ten ducat gold coin from inside his jacket and slips it into my purse. Bewildered, I make no reaction. With a tilt of his head he takes out another of the same coins. He adds that to the first and then he takes my wrist and starts to lead me towards the back doors.

It's only then I understand what's happening and my legs go so weak that I can hardly walk. With a surge of lust, I realise that I've just sold myself to him for twenty ducats and, now, he's taking me outside to have me.

He escorts me out through a doorway into the darkness and a servant comes over to meet us, carrying a guttering lantern. My 'client' gives him some coins and he beckons us to follow him.

Just for the night of the ball, a long line of partitioned wooden booths has been built against the side of the warehouse. There are some twenty of them, like a row of horse's stalls, only smaller. They're roughly made, even lacking doors, only made private by a hanging curtain.

The roofs are open as well and, as we walk down in front of the occupied booths, the air is alive with moans and groans and the sound of naked bodies slapping together. It's very erotic, especially as I know it can't be long now before my own cries will be mingling with all the others.

We come to an empty booth. My lover-to-be politely gestures me in ahead of him. There's nothing in the booth except for a very deep, waist-height shelf that fills the whole of the back of the booth.

It's obvious what I have to do. I turn to sit on the shelf and then I lie back down. There's just enough space for the man to follow me into the booth and drop the curtain closed behind him.

Urgent with desire, he takes hold of my ankles and lifts them up. I haven't noticed before but, level with his shoulders, there are loops of sacking fixed to both walls. He slips each of my feet through the loop on either side of him and then releases his grasp to leave me held in a comfortable, though extremely vulgar, position. It's very dark in the booth, but I know he must be well aware my ripe quim is split wide open in front of him.

I see his dark shape loom over me. His hands go to my toga, pulling it up over my breasts. I want him to enter me straight away but, to my confusion, his shadow slowly drops away, sinking downwards.

Shockingly, I feel his head sliding between my legs. The edges of his mask press into my inner thighs and then, a moment later, his tongue is on me. He's actually pushing it out through the mouth hole in his mask and licking the nub of my clitoris with the tip of it.

Whenever I've heard of this forbidden act I've always been told it's only ever the very loosest of harlots that will allow any man to perform it upon her. I should be horrified that he's doing it to me, but I'm not. My strongest emotion is delirious excitement at how big my clitoris feels. The way his probing tongue is lapping at me is making it enormous.

More than anything else I feel absolutely disgraced by the knowledge it's going to make me come so very, very quickly. I start to arch back almost immediately. I'm transported by his constant tonguing. I can't help thinking of how he must be drinking in my honey juices, tasting my quim in his mouth. It's only going to take a few more licks and I'll be there. I'm right on the edge now.

And then, without warning, he stops.

I can hardly believe it. He lifts away from me just as I'm about to climax, leaving me aching for release. He stands again and, unbuttoning his jacket and shirt, he says, 'I'm afraid you'll have to wait a little while longer. I don't intend to bring you to pleasure just yet, I only wanted to test how much of a wanton you really are.'

His top clothes are off now and I'm surprised at how much thinner he looks without their padding. He slides his boots off and then he begins unbuttoning his trousers.

'I'm pleased you're so aroused because you'll need to be. I have to tell you that I can only achieve real satisfaction when I mount a woman in a very special way. No lady would ever consider entertaining my desires, so I only can only ever truly satiate myself upon whores like yourself.'

He steps out of his trousers and stands in front of me. By this time my eyes have got more used to the dark and I can make him out more clearly.

I soon get to find out what his 'special way' is. I see he would be completely naked now if it wasn't for a belt he's wearing strapped round his upper thigh. Looking at it I see why he needed to wear his trousers so loose. He's been walking around all evening with his hugely long cock strapped down to the inside of his leg. But there is something else much worse to come.

When he releases the thin strap that's holding his shaft down so tightly, his erection twists round to rear up in front of him and it's only then that I see that the whole length of it is sheathed in a tube of raised leather. The bulbous head of his cock is pushing out of a sleeve of ribbed rings that's tied round his testicles and capped with a tab of rough fur. It's just like the one I found in Mario's desk!

For the first time I really stare through the darkness towards the masked man in front of me and the truth finally sinks in. I begin to recognise the shape of his head, the set of his shoulders – the man is Mario!

In a flash, I see it all. No wonder Mario was so flustered when I stumbled on the sleeve in his desk. It was his all along! That whole story he'd told me was just a pack of lies. The only erection this tube has ever been pushed onto is his own! How clever it was of him to trick me into thinking he'd burnt it.

Even though I'm completely devastated to learn that my seemingly prudish husband is really a perverted whorer, for the moment I have to put all that to the back of my mind.

If Mario were to discover that it is me lying here, upturned with my legs hung open ready for fornicating intercourse, it is I who will be ruined. I would be found out, not only as a shameless adulteress, but also as a lustful slut who thinks so much of her prowess she demands twice the going rate for her services. I must do nothing that would give myself away. I have no choice but to carry on just as though I really am the prostitute he believes me to be. I must not raise his suspicions by refusing his demands.

He's moving in between my thighs now. I try to behave just as I imagine any real whore would and tilt myself slightly to make his entry more easy.

Wearing the sleeve obviously excites him very much. He's incredibly erect, the slick tip of his cock is thrusting right out of the end of the tube. He touches it against my vulva lips and starts to guide himself into me. I grip the edge of the shelf and brace myself.

The ball of purple flesh slides in easily enough, but then, when he starts to push the girth of the sleeve in after it, I feel it opening me up, wider and then wider still. I begin to wonder if my tight little 'lady's' quim is going to be able to take him.

Doing nothing more than pressing against me, he very slowly forces the whole length of the sleeve up inside me. My quim jolts involuntarily as each raised ring enters me. The leather feels just as cruelly cold and hard inside me as I had imagined it.

As he sinks to the hilt I feel my clitoris being rasped against the fur tab, stimulated by a thousand tiny pin-pricks of sensation. I want to make some sort of noise, but I have to stifle the sounds. The thing feels absolutely huge inside me.

He pulls back and then presses forward again. And then out and in again. Faster now. Faster again, getting his rhythm. My fingers are clenching so hard they're turning white. He's going so fast now he's making the muscles of my sex vibrate as he continually ribs me open with the rings. I've never experienced anything like this in my whole life. I can hardly stand it.

The vibrations travel through me, making my legs quiver. I hear my feet start to beat against the walls. I can't hold my moans back. I have to let them out, but I have to do it disguising my voice so he won't recognise me. It makes them so low and husky they sound really filthy and that just spurs him on to go even harder.

The noise of our lovemaking is exciting the couples in the booths near us. I can hear the sounds of their coupling getting louder as they get more and more aroused listening to us. My pulsing movements are making the walls of the booth shake. I'm loving it now. I start to arch back further, gasping out through bitten lips. I've reached the point of no return. Even if he pulled out now I'd still climax. I clearly hear the woman in the next booth exclaim aloud, 'My God! What is he doing to her in there?' and the jealousy in her voice excites me so much it brings my orgasm on.

I start to grunt like an animal. The glow of pleasure floods out from my quim in waves. I start to jerk each time he goes into me. I'm coming. With my sex stretched tight over the whole of that obscene leather tube, I'm coming.

Seeing me climax so strongly sends Mario wild. He takes hold of my hips and pumps himself into me urgently, working into me again and again until, suddenly, he's jerking too.

He starts to jet inside me and I'm so open I can feel his come spilling into me in great gushes.

We fall apart exhausted. Totally unaware of my true identity, my own husband has ridden me like a randy whore. That shameful sex toy of his has taken me to the most incredible orgasm I've ever had, but he'll never find out that it was really me.

When he leaves here he'll never know that the woman he's just mounted in such a lewd way was, in fact, his own respectable wife. But I know his secret now and that gives me power. The next time Mario comes to my bed things will be very different.

Chapter 5

Sadly, there is little hope that I will ever make such a discovery about my own husband. But, just as it seems I must resign myself to unhappiness, it is then that Fate comes to my rescue and presents me with the opportunity to slake my growing thirst for sexual pleasure – albeit in the most immoral and disgraceful of ways.

It begins with an unforeseen death. My cousin, who is only thirty, is killed in a tragic riding accident. We were very close when we were younger and, before she got married, she often used to visit our home. She had had a very unlucky life – her cavalry officer husband had been cut down in battle less than six months after their honeymoon. That was nearly three years ago and I had not seen much of her since then, only knowing that soon afterwards she had sold up and moved to a new house on the far side of Angers.

Although her death is an awful shock what is even more unexpected is the discovery that she has left this town house to me in her will.

The first morning after all the ceremonies of her funeral are completed I make arrangements for one of Charles's coachmen to drive me the ten or so miles into Angers to view my new inheritance. On the way I think to myself that, as I have little use for the house, I would be sensible to sell it at the first opportunity.

As we arrive I make to open the carriage door but, suddenly, from out of nowhere, a small boy appears in front of me, thrusts a sealed letter into my hands and then runs off again. Bewildered, I read the flowing handwriting that's penned across it, *'To Madame Sancerre from Beatrice Raymond. For her private reading.'*

I'm more than a little taken aback by this. Even I know that Beatrice Raymond is the madam of what is politely known as the town's 'hostel for single ladies'. Her clientele and the goings on there are a constant source of gossip to the servants.

It is only when I think of it now I realise that, although facing different streets, the grounds of my cousin's house and Madame Raymond's 'hostel' actually back onto one another.

I tuck the letter inside my shawl, keeping it safely hidden until I am alone inside the house.

Then, full of curiosity, I open it to read,

Dear Madame Sancerre,

Please excuse me for communicating with you in this unusual manner, but as it concerns a matter of some delicacy, I am sure you would prefer it is dealt with as discreetly as possible.

I believe that you are now to be the new owner of your cousin's house, God rest her soul. Although I fear it may distress you, it is vitally important that you learn from me alone that for some time your cousin and I had been involved in a highly confidential business arrangement. This arrangement required that a doorway was knocked through between the wine cellars that extend beneath the back of our two properties so she could come and go in secrecy without attracting unwanted attention.

The Pleasure Ring

Being sure that you will wish this doorway to be sealed before it is discovered by persons who might reveal its existence to others, may I humbly suggest that we meet down in the cellars immediately so that you can inspect the work that will be required to close it off.

I am sorry to have to also inform you that your cousin passed away owing me a large amount of money for certain works I carried out on her behalf. Perhaps we could also discuss this when we meet?

Yours Beatrice Raymond

I have never been to my cousin's house before but, even so, it does not take me long to find a candle holder and uncover the cellar entrance. Holding the light before me, I descend steep, stone steps into a vaulted, brick room lined with wooden wine racks. A second cellar, just the same, opens out from the far end of the first and beyond that a third one. As I grope my way into this last room I discern a thin crack of light glimmering from behind the furthermost wooden rack. Realising this must be the private doorway, I edge between the shelving and the wall to get through to it, my full skirt brushing cobwebs from the dusty bottles lying on the racks as I squeeze by. Just as I reach the door, Madam Raymond pushes it open and beckons me across the threshold.

The cellar I emerge into is laid out in almost exactly the same way as my cousin's, but the three rooms are furnished very differently. The wine racks have all been removed and each of the rooms has been divided off by wooden walls and doorways. Candles burn brightly from half a dozen or more stands, bathing the bare-floored cellars in light.

The only feature that catches my attention is that on one side of the doorway between this cellar and the next, a large circular opening has been cut through the wall. It's been made just above the level of a peculiar kind of high couch that's standing out from the wall in front of it. The hole has been fitted with a heavy canvas collar that has drawstrings laced through it so that it can be drawn closed into the centre, shutting off the other room. The couch underneath the hole is built very strongly and the surface is covered all over with deep velvet padding but, strangest of all, at the outer two corners there are buckled leather cuffs chained to the wooden frame.

It's only when I realise that the cuffs are designed for restraining someone's wrists that it begins to dawn on me what this strange piece of equipment really is. And who it was made for.

When Madame Raymond sees the look on my face her relief is obvious. 'I am most pleased that you have already half guessed what the purpose of the couch is for, Madame Sancerre. It makes my task so very much easier. But, please, do not be so shocked, my dear. Your cousin was widowed so very young. She was still a passionate young woman, still filled with sexual urges. It was never going to be possible for her to marry again, but she couldn't bear the thought of all the long years that lay ahead of her and never feeling the pleasure of having a man inside her again.

'It was she who came to me with the plans for the opening you see before you; her idea to have it arranged so that she could lie on the couch and push the bottom half of her body through the hole into the next room. With the canvas collar tied tightly round her waist and her head and shoulders sealed on this side of the wall no one on the other side would ever be able to uncover her true identity. She could retain her reputation whilst being serviced by as many men as I could provide.

'Wanting to help her, I went to great expense to install all

The Pleasure Ring

the features she desired. Sadly though, her scheme was not a success. She only ever used the couch three times. You see, madam, she wasn't able to cope with the intensity of the experience of presenting herself so helplessly. She was so disturbed by the emotions it aroused that, right from the start, it was clear she was going to have to be tied and gagged to stop her breaking free and betraying herself by calling out. The three sessions she submitted herself to nearly broke her. She was always promising to return so that I could earn back some of the money I'd spent out, but she could never bring herself to do it.'

I try to listen to Madame Raymond's words but I can hardly take them in. Ever since she'd confirmed my wild imaginings about the opening, an insane idea has been forming in my head. A plan so frightening it scares me. And yet so exciting I can't contain it. I blurt it out to her now, even as I speak dreading that she might not turn me down.

'Madam, I will gladly undertake to pay back the debt you are owed. I will give you money if that is what you wish, but perhaps it could suit us both much better if you allowed me to settle the sum in another way. How can I say it, "in kind".' I look over to the opening as I speak to her, leaving her in no doubt as to my meaning.

Madame Raymond is not only a good businesswoman, she is also most experienced in matters of sexual desire. She'd seen my expression when I'd guessed what the opening was really for and had recognised the barely concealed look of lust on my face. She agrees to my proposition at once and we begin discussing the way it might be accomplished without further delay.

In fact, it takes surprisingly little time to arrange everything. I tell Charles that I have changed my mind about selling the house and that I now intend to use it as a place of my own for painting and studying. I say to him that I have found many interesting books in my cousin's library that I would like to read to improve my mind. And I honestly believe he is more than glad that I have found a pastime that will get me away from the estate and leave him free to go hunting even more often.

One afternoon, less than a fortnight later, I have myself taken back to the house again for what is to be my initiation on the couch. As soon as I arrive I send the coachman away with strict orders not to disturb me again until the early evening. The moment he leaves I go down to the cellar and make my way through the connecting door. Beatrice, as I now call her, is already waiting for me in the end room.

In nervous silence I let her help me out of my clothes and then lead me, naked, over to the couch. Trembling a little already, I climb up onto it and insert my legs and waist through the hole until my feet drop down to touch the floor on the other side, in the middle cellar. She quickly draws the canvas collar closed and knots it tightly round the narrowest part of my belly. I allow her to lock my wrists into the cuffs and, with a few final words of encouragement, she winds a long silk scarf round my head and gags me mute.

Now I'm ready, it's time for Beatrice to leave me and go to prepare my first visitor, a trusted client of old. Taking the candle, she locks the door behind her and I'm left in total darkness. A little pillow has been placed on the couch by my head and I rest my cheek on it as I wait with pounding heart, knowing the last chance for turning back has just slipped away.

I have the pleasure ring in place and I can feel my clitoris pulsing inside its grip. I'm reminded of when I first showed it to Beatrice, how her only reaction was to brush her hand

The Pleasure Ring

affectionately against my cheek. She told me then that now she thought she understood why my cousin had left the house to me; that it must have been that she'd seen something inside me that told her I would make good use of her secret.

On the other side of the wall there are two small stools fixed to the floor below the opening. I have the choice of either standing or kneeling with a leg on each stool. But, as some sort of sexual forfeit she made herself pay, my cousin had deliberately set the stools just far enough apart that she could only rest on them by daring to split her thighs wide open and pushing her bottom up high into the air. It frightens me to offer my sex out like that, but my legs feel so weak I don't think they'll support me if I try to remain standing. I have no choice but to move onto the stools and exhibit myself completely. I'm shaking like a leaf now, dreading what's going to happen, yet at the same time I can feel the wetness dripping out of me. My nipples are so hard I have to rasp them up and down the rough cord of the velvet to ease the pain.

After an eternity I hear footsteps descending the stairs. It's Beatrice's man, coming down into the far cellar to undress before opening the door into the middle room.

And now I know the fear my cousin felt. If there were any way I could do it I'd tear the scarf off and shout at the top of my voice for Beatrice to come and set me free, plead and beg the man not to touch me. I'm so vulnerable, so completely exposed. He's going to be able to do anything he wants to me and there's nothing I can do to stop him.

I hear the door opening. What must I look like to him? Just my bare legs pushed into the empty room. No hands to restrict him, only the hard globes of my arse lifted up and presented to him, drawn apart to reveal the moist folds of my pouting sex glinting in the flickering candlelight.

He treads across the room. I know he'll be nude apart from a waxed silk seed-catcher tied round his waist with a satin ribbon. I imagine his already hard, erect cock encased in it, standing out of him; wagging up and down like a spear as he walks towards me.

He draws near and I hear him moan softly as he spies the pleasure ring nestling between my labia. The first touch comes without warning. A fingertip gently brushes over my lips and I jolt from head to foot, jerking against my bonds, body rigid with tension. Even through the wall I can sense his arousal at the sight of the golden band, how much it's making him want me.

He moves behind me and spreads me open. The creased seam of the sheath tip grazes between my lips and I scream silently into the gag. A moment's pause and then we groan in unison as he slowly skewers the full length of his shaft into me.

It begins now.

And it's pure and utter bliss.

With practised skill the unseen, unknown man takes command and I can do nothing more than lie there whimpering on the end of his cock as he rides me firmly and masterfully to a shattering orgasm. My submission is total. He delivers me to such a climax that all the pent-up tension and apprehension I'd felt before floods out of me in a great wave of ecstasy. The power of it overwhelms me completely, leaves me clinging to the couch like a shipwrecked mariner washed up after a storm.

That first time I only have one visitor, but then I never look back. Before long I'm travelling to the house three

The Pleasure Ring

times a week, offering myself through the opening to six or even seven men in succession. And, because of the ring, I come with every single one of them. I'm totally insatiable. When I'm there on the table I become a completely different personality – a shameless, promiscuous slut who craves nothing more than to be pleasured. This other me has no interest in love and tenderness, her only desire is to be brought to violent orgasm, again and again.

She even has her own story, for I have arranged with Beatrice to say to all the men that, really, I am a woman who has failed to repay a debt to her. She has to tell them that I have reluctantly agreed to work off my debt in the cellar like this but, because I have displeased her, she wants me to be taught a lesson. The men must show me no affection, there is to be no touching or foreplay. They are told they must come into the room and take me immediately, to be as strong and forceful as they can; not spare me at all. I have had leather reins fixed to the wall for them to grip onto so that they can pull themselves into me harder, stirrups hung from the stools for them to step into and saddle me deeper still.

Now, when a man comes through the door, I just love knowing he's longing to caress me, kiss my sex, finger the pleasure ring, but that he has to restrain himself, hold back because of Beatrice's strict commands. I love the way he has no choice but to stride across the room and take me straight away as he's been instructed. It excites me because I know the frustration he feels just makes him want to mount me all the harder.

I never lose the spine-tingling chill that runs through me as I wait in the blackness to hear that door opening, but I soon discover the strange fact that being deprived of my sight seems to make all my other senses grow all the more acute. After a while, I even find that, just by the sound of their footsteps and the noises the men make when they are pleasuring themselves upon me, I can actually recognise many of them. Quite a few are friends of my husband. Can you imagine what a feeling of power it gives me if I get the chance to meet these men again in the evening? To stand there in polite conversation with them, my sex still throbbing from the ferocity of their penetration. To talk innocently with them, knowing they have absolutely no idea that, just a few hours ago, it was *me* they stole away from their wives for and rutted with so savagely, in so animal a way.

The next six months are the happiest I've ever known. In my secret double life, my sexual needs are being completely satisfied. Every week I'm brought to orgasm by twenty or more different men. In addition, the debt that my cousin owed is long paid off and now Beatrice is sharing with me the profits she makes from all the men who come from far and wide for the experience of mounting her mystery harlot who offers herself so lewdly. For the first time in my life, I've been able to save up a little sum of money of my own.

My only mistake is to believe that it could ever last.

At the end of one especially vigorous session I hear the cellar door being opened for the last time that day. As always, I listen to the pad of bare feet crossing the room, but, on this occasion, my heightened sense of hearing picks up something different about it.

I can't help thinking the footfalls are particularly light. It isn't the tread of a grown man; it must be someone quite young. There's another thing, as well. I can tell the man has undressed because there is no rustling of clothes, but there's an odd sound – the faintest jangle of chains.

I hear him stopping directly behind me. For a few

The Pleasure Ring

seconds there's no movement, then hands touch on my back, stroking gently down to cup my buttocks before trailing lower to massage my thighs. This man is breaking all the rules, flagrantly fondling me even though he must have been told that it is absolutely forbidden.

The touch is delicate, fingertips smooth and fine. In my mind I see a youth, maybe seventeen or eighteen, perhaps on his very first visit to Madam Raymond's house. I imagine how he has been overcome with excitement at finding me presented like this, how he can't resist going against all he's been told for the chance of exploring a woman in a way he's never been able to before. I feel a little spark of arousal at the thought of his virile, virgin cock pulsing in his silk sheath as he moves his hands over me. For a moment I have the vision of the sight of me being too much for him and hearing him groaning in despair as he loses control and starts to fill the end of his seed-catcher with an over-eager boy's come before he's even touched it against my sex.

And yet, that doesn't seem right. His movements are too assured, too experienced in the subtle art of exciting the female body. I find myself being tantalisingly stimulated as he begins circling his hands over me, visiting every part of my thighs except for my clitoris. He works nearer and ever nearer until I feel my nub swelling out through the ring, yearning to be touched.

Then, at long last, the hands slide in between my legs to part my sex lips. I sigh deeply as the probing fingertips find me, but that isn't the end of my torment. For the man does no more than mock me by milking the hardness of my clitoris like a teat, testing the slick wetness he finds there and exposing my want.

The fingers slip away, content that I have been made ready. I'm sure I hear the same muted jangle of chain again, this time mingled with a high, barely stifled moan. Then a hand slides onto my sex once more and I'm opened up, peeled apart in preparation for penetration.

I feel his cock tip touching me. But it's not right! It's cold and hard. Not real.

It's a dildo! A huge, smooth, porcelain dildo!

And now I realise the truth.

It's not a man at all. It's a woman!

I'm helpless to do anything as the impostor begins to sink the great mushroom-shaped head of the dildo inside me, bearing forward to push the stalk-like shaft in behind. It goes right into me until the rough mat of her damp pubis presses hard up against mine. Slowly, she eases the dildo back and then presses it home again. Then again, and again, stroking it in and out of me.

I can tell something else now too. The way she jerks a little every time she forces the shaft into me. The way I can feel her pressing tight against me, with only the sensation of two thin chains denting into the flesh of our thighs as they splash together. The way the dildo seems to be held so rigidly. It can only mean one thing.

The dildo she's using on me is double-ended. She must have it hung from some sort of belt round her waist, a curving arc of twin-headed phallus suspended from its centre on those two lengths of chain. The moan I heard was her inserting the other end into her own sex. And now we're sharing it. She's penetrating herself with just as much force as she's entering me. Every time she pushes forward our labias kiss together so tightly I swear I can feel the hard pea of her clitoris dimpling into me.

She starts to work the palms of both hands in between our slapping vulvas. One hand below the dildo to my clitoris, the other above it to her own. I can't help being

The Pleasure Ring

excited. This is such a shameful act of intimacy. We're joined together, stimulating each other, straddled on the same cock phallus, our bodies mated in a way that only two women can ever share together.

I know it's going to make me come, but she doesn't make it easy for me. No one but another woman would know how to take me so close to climax and yet hold me back from release.

Once, twice, three times she takes me right to the very edge and brings me back, brushing her fingertips over me with a feather-light teasing that drives me wild. I want to orgasm so badly, now. I twist and rub against her, frantically trying to catch her out, to make her touch me too hard and accidentally take me over the brink.

I know she's having trouble controlling her own excitement now, too. I can feel her thrusting getting more and more erratic, hear her short, panting breaths, feel her struggling against the need of her body.

Suddenly her fingers become urgent. She starts to rub hard with both hands. I feel the coming welling up from my clitoris, know there won't be, can't be, any going back this time.

She falls forward against me and we climax simultaneously, quivering together as we suffer the sensations of each other's orgasmic convulsions pulsing backwards and forwards through the jerking dildo.

Now, the rapture of orgasm has ebbed away, I feel the woman stirring again. She lifts herself from me, but it's only so that she can move closer to the canvas collar and whisper, 'You enjoyed that, didn't you, Amande?'

I pale to hear my name spoken in this place. But worse, that voice, I know that voice!

It's Angel!

I start to struggle against my bonds, straining uselessly to free myself, and I hear her laugh. 'You recognise me now, don't you, Amande? But I knew it was you all along. Ever since you ran out on me so rudely that night at the opera I've had my spies keep track of you. At first, it seemed you'd married some boring old country squire and I lost interest. But then, I started to hear reports of a sensational new whore in Angers who stood with her minge pushed through a hole in the brothel wall so that no man might know her true identity. I was intrigued and impressed. All the more so when they told me this half-concealed wanton wore a gold ring round her clitoris and I realised it could only be you.

'That pleased me greatly because I thought I'd badly misjudged you. It's always nice to know I haven't lost my ability to spot a slut – especially one as well hidden as the sweet little innocent you had everybody else believing you were.

'I knew it was you, but I wanted to come and see for myself. I wanted to find out just how good a harlot I'd made of you. I rather enjoyed dressing up as a man and fooling your madam into letting me in here. And, as you well know now, I came with my disguise complete right down to the most important detail. It seemed such a waste to hand over all that money for you and not get what I paid for. I don't think you minded too much though, did you?

'In fact, you were so good I really think I must write to your husband to congratulate him on how excellent a whore his wife actually is. Don't you think that would be a good idea, Amande?

'You see, my dear, I've got a lot of time on my hands for correspondence like that at the moment. Things have got a little too hot for me in Paris and I really need to get away – to travel. But it is *so* expensive and I haven't

The Pleasure Ring

got anything like the money I need to live the way I'm used to.

'Of course, if by some chance someone like yourself was kind enough to give me the sort of sum I'm looking for, then I'd be able to leave straight away. And, do you know, I'd be gone so quickly I feel sure I'd completely forget about unimportant things like writing letters.'

I understand her meaning all too well, but before she leaves me spells the terms of her blackmail out even more clearly. In return for my agreement to give her one hundred crowns, virtually all my savings, she swears, on her life, that she will send no letter to Charles.

The arrangement is simple. The next day that I visit the town house I have the money with me when I arrive. Just after my own carriage has left, another with all the blinds drawn tight pulls up outside. The driver jumps down and comes to the door, holding his hand out. I pass the heavy purse of coins to him and, without even the slightest nod of thanks, he turns and climbs back into his seat.

As he spurs the horses off down the street towards the highroad I stand and watch until they are completely out of view. Only then do I enter the house, praying with all my heart that this moment will be the last time I ever see or hear of Angel.

I light my candle and make my way down to the cellar to pass through to Beatrice's. I'm a little early and she's not there to meet me yet. I close the connecting door behind me, glad of a few moments' peace to compose myself.

But as I sit alone in the shadowy glow of the single candle I begin to feel strangely uneasy. The feeling grows and grows until, all at once, I'm gripped by the most powerful foreboding of danger. A danger so close it's making the hairs on the back of my neck stand on end.

All my instincts scream to me to get out of the room. In a blind panic I rush to the door to get back to my own house and safety.

But it's too late. Before I can escape, the door to the middle room suddenly bursts off its hinges with a terrible splintering of timber and the angry, looming shape of my husband is silhouetted in the doorway by the lights of many lamps.

He lunges at me and then drags me roughly by the arm back into the middle cellar. I see Beatrice there as well, being held against her will by two men. Others are with them but, standing alone by the opening, examining the straps and stools below it with an expression of perfect disgust, is the black-robed figure of the local priest.

I laugh out loud at my own stupidity. The priest is holding a letter in his hand – a letter from Angel. I see it all now. Angel has played me for a fool once again. The vow she made so sincerely only ever promised never to send a letter to Charles. And what would he have done with it? No doubt he would have confronted me and bitter words would have been spoken, but it would have remained a secret between us. Charles would have made sure of that. What man would want to announce to the world that his wife has been had by half the men in town behind his back?

But, by sending the letter to the priest, Angel had cleverly made sure that now the whole business will be completely exposed. She's deliberately betrayed me to the Church knowing that they, of all people, will punish me the most severely for my sins.

There is little point in denying the accusations she's made about me. All the evidence is here for them to see. I'm immediately found guilty of the charges brought against me and now it only remains for the priest to decide my fate.

Chapter 6

By one of those chance coincidences that shape all our lives, it so happens that, on that very day, the powerful Abbot of Poitiers is due to pay a visit to the priest on his way back to his Abbey. The priest is known to be an ambitious man and I am sure he sees an opportunity of gaining favour by humbly seeking the Abbot's advice on the matter of my sentencing.

When the Abbot arrives I am brought before him. He is an imposing figure, a fit, steely-eyed man, more like a soldier than a man of God. But, for all the priest's trouble, the Abbot seems remarkably uninterested in my case and does not even lower himself to speak to me directly. Instead, he instructs the priest to question me a second time whilst he listens without bothering to conceal his boredom. Only after he's heard all the evidence does he lean over and whisper gravely to the priest behind his hand before getting up and leaving the room without so much as glancing at me again. It is left to the priest to announce that, because of the seriousness of the depravities I have confessed to, the Abbot has decided to take the task of my punishment upon himself. Initially, I am to make a pilgrimage to the monastery at Poitiers on foot and then, when I arrive, I will be informed as to what further penitence I must undertake.

The Abbot rides for Poitiers the next day, but he leaves behind a letter for me; a note of absolution that I am instructed to hand to the host monk of the pilgrims' lodging house at the Abbey as soon as I arrive there. The Abbot will sign the note when I have completed my penitence to his satisfaction and then I will be able to bring it back with me as proof to the priest that I have been cleansed of my sins.

I leave for Poitiers as soon as I can. I know I'm not safe now until I have the note signed. Without absolution I'm a marked woman – a sinner that the priest and the Church can do almost whatever they like with.

Although the pilgrims' way to Poitiers passes within a few miles of Angers, it crosses long stretches of lonely forest land soon afterwards. I've been warned it's safer to travel in groups, so when I meet the path I wait until a band of pilgrims passes by and then ask to join them.

The walking this first day is hard. We have to reach the next rest house before dusk and it's quite some way on. There's not much chance to talk to anyone, but I don't mind too much. Almost for the first time in days I get a chance to be alone with my thoughts.

I keep going over in my head the remark Angel had made after she'd brought me to orgasm so shamefully in Beatrice's cellar. The things she'd said about being glad she hadn't misjudged me and being so pleased she hadn't been wrong about the slut in me. I realise now it hadn't been my body that had excited her; it was finding me giving myself so wantonly and knowing it was she who had first recognised the waywardness inside me and guided me down the road of corruption.

And I also see clearly now that I wasn't the first sexually eager young girl who had fallen into her clutches.

Once, in Paris, she'd told me a tale about a maid of hers.

The Pleasure Ring

At the time I thought it had just been an amusing story she'd made up to impress me, but now I realise it had been the truth and that she'd recounted it as a boast of her skill.

The story had started when Angel was staying at her sister's country house for a grand party. Some time in the morning afterwards, she had returned to her room to collect her shawl just as the chambermaid was about to make the bed.

The maid had carried on working, turning the covers down, but the moment she exposed the bottom sheet she let out a gasp of shocked embarrassment.

The whole of the white linen sheet was completely splattered with trails of semen stains!

Angel didn't say it in as many words, but she led me to understand that, after the party, she'd been entertaining six young army cadets in her room for the night. Of course, they'd all wanted to have her, but she'd denied them all. Instead she'd forced them to stand round the bed touching themselves whilst she displayed herself masturbating in all kinds of different poses. Time and time again, she'd made them shoot their seed all over her breasts and thighs and buttocks until, by dawn, she'd been almost covered in come.

I imagine the look on the chambermaid's face was exactly the same as my expression when I first saw that serving girl sink herself down on the drinker at the inn at Fontainebleau – that same mixture of wide-eyed astonishment and unschooled lust. It may only have been there for a second, but it was long enough for Angel to notice it. And long enough to seal the girl's fate.

The challenge of leading the girl astray was too much of a temptation for Angel to resist. As soon as she returned downstairs she asked her sister if she might borrow the maid whilst her own servant made a journey home to visit a sick relation. Aware of Angel's reputation even then, her sister was most reluctant to let the girl go, but was eventually persuaded to let her decide for herself. Much to the sister's surprise the maid agreed at once. Though, needless to say, to Angel that was just further confirmation of what she'd seen in the girl's face.

The very day they arrived back in Paris, Angel set her plans in motion by giving the girl the task of filling a hip bath for her in front of the fire in her bedroom.

Like everyone else, Angel knew full well that it is regarded as improper for servants to ever see their master or mistress in a state of undress. But that day she made a point of parading herself round half naked before she got in the water. The red-faced girl did her best to keep her eyes averted to the floor, but Angel wasn't going to let her get away so lightly.

Once she was in the bath, she sent the maid on an errand to fetch another jug of hot water. The young girl nearly spilt it all over herself when she returned to find Angel standing by her bed in the nude, with one leg lifted up on the covers. She was supposed to be anointing her sex with powder, but she was using the pad so firmly the whole of her rosy pink, just-bathed vulva was plainly quivering with sensation.

Angel made no secret to the maid that she often had men to stay for the night. When the girl brought up her breakfast tray any morning afterwards, she deliberately taunted her by letting herself be discovered looking exhausted from hours of abandoned lovemaking.

Now, there was a huge wooden wardrobe in Angel's bedroom that stood against the wall opposite her four-poster bed. Both the doors on this wardrobe were pierced with holes to let air circulate around the clothes inside, but there was a square of black cloth fixed against the inside of each of them that acted as a kind of screen. It was only a short time after the maid had arrived that Angel noticed that the top corner of one of these screens had been carefully folded back and she realised her scheme was working better than she could ever have hoped.

The next time she went out expecting to bring a 'friend' back for the night, she made sure the maid knew all about it. And then, although this sounds odd, just before she left for the evening she sprinkled a dusting of powder on the floor in front of the wardrobe.

When she returned with the man some time after midnight, they immediately lay on the bed and began kissing and caressing passionately. After a while Angel broke away and urged the man to undress and move under the sheets whilst she got out of her own clothes. In the most natural way, she slipped off the bed and walked across the room carrying a candlestick in her hand. She made sure she passed close to the wardrobe and as she did so she looked down to find exactly what she'd suspected. There was a trail of bare footprints in the powder – footprints leading straight to the wardrobe!

The maid was hiding in there, waiting to spy on Angel and the man coupling on the bed!

Angel quickly cast her clothes off and jerked the bedclothes back. Quite taken aback by the unexpected force of her own arousal, she sat astride the man and mounted him vigorously in full view of the wardrobe; knowing she was giving the maid a perfect picture of her sex spiking up and down on the man's prick. And as she rode him she leant forward and whispered in his ear the secret of their hidden voyeur. She swore to me that the man's cock grew an extra inch when he heard of the maid's impudent act.

The two of them put on the most erotic display, mating energetically in all manner of elaborate positions designed to excite the girl.

When they'd finally spent themselves, Angel discreetly blew out the last of the candles and drew the curtains round the sides of the bed. Though she made sure to leave a little gap next to her head so that she could look out into the room.

She lay awake, waiting, for half an hour or so and then, at last, her patience was rewarded when the door of the wardrobe silently opened and the maid stepped out into the room. As the girl tiptoed out of the servant's door, Angel saw that she was wearing nothing more than a pair of silken knickers. She smiled when she noticed how the crotch was soaked through where it had been ruched up into the folds of her vulva, realising at once that the resourceful girl had been masturbating herself through the material to quieten the sound of her fingers slapping between her wet labia lips.

At the time of the story, Angel was keeping a stable of no fewer than a dozen men who visited her regularly. It goes without saying that she wasn't sharing her favours with these 'friends' for free; each of them had to show their appreciation with some small gift of jewellery or money. Word soon spread amongst these men about the maid and her spying place and soon they all wanted to perform for her. And they all wanted to outdo the others.

From then onwards the girl was treated to the nightly spectacle of watching Angel being taken in the most breathtakingly lewd ways. And, each time, Angel would lie awake to watch her leave, always noting how she never wore anything other than the same pair of scanty drawers.

For a while Angel was happy to play along with the maid's game. It aroused her to be watched and the men were

The Pleasure Ring

willing to pay a great deal extra for this new diversion. But when the novelty began to wear off, she suddenly decided to change the rules. The maid must have been very surprised the night that Angel returned with not one, but eight men!

As soon as the door was closed behind them, Angel stripped down to her underwear and started to pour wine for them all as they undressed as well. There was a real air of anticipation and soon the men were very erect. It was quite crowded for them all in the small room, especially now that every one of them was carrying around that long, plum-tipped spear of muscle between their legs. Angel had laughed when she recalled how they had all been so very careful not to accidentally probe each other's buttocks as they moved about.

Then, suddenly, Angel gave a signal and the men lined themselves up in a semi-circle around the wardrobe. They all stood facing it with their hard cocks pointing towards the poor girl. She was like a prisoner in front of a firing squad. There was no doubt the game was over now!

One of the men stepped forward to turn the door handle, but Angel quickly beckoned him back. Instead she called to the girl, 'I know you're in there and I know what you've been doing.

'But now I've caught you, I can't help feeling it's all been too easy. I've had so little sport from this that I've decided to throw in a kind of gamble – a way of letting Chance decide if you're to be spared the fate these young men have planned for you.

'Now, listen carefully. This is the wager! I'm going to count to ten and then I want you to come out so that we can all see you. I swear that if you're wearing any clothing then you'll be free to leave and this night will never be mentioned again. However, if it turns out that you're naked, then I can't answer for what might happen to you before morning. I really don't think I can be any fairer than that now, can I? Be ready, I'm starting the count!'

Immediately there was the sound of frantic movement inside the wardrobe and all the men turned to stare at Angel angrily. They couldn't believe what she'd done. They'd all been expecting, even half promised, that the maid would be given to them that night and now Angel had cheated them by offering the girl an easy way to escape.

But Angel kept her nerve and carried on counting slowly until she reached ten. For a few moments there was silence and then, very hesitantly, the door swung open and the maid stepped out – completely naked!

This had been the whole point of Angel's story. The men had all imagined the noise they had heard from the wardrobe was the bare maid desperately trying to find some item of clothing to pull on. But Angel had known better. She'd known that over the weeks she'd filled the girl so full of want that she couldn't walk away now, even when the chance was offered.

Angel knew the truth, that displaying herself so lasciviously had excited the young woman so much that she'd actually been tearing her pants off in her lustful desire to be taken the same way.

Her wish was soon granted too. One of the men took her hand and gently led her over to the bed and then they fell on her like a pack of wild animals.

And when I think of it now, I imagine Angel watching her from the shadows, leaning back against the wall, masturbating triumphantly as the girl's cries echo round the room.

Chapter 7

No matter how long I spend going over the past, I know I can't make any plans for the future until I get this tiresome business in Poitiers out of the way. I decide to keep my distance from the others, wanting to attract as little attention to myself as possible.

There are three other women in the party; two of them walk alone, plainly feeling the same as I do, but I can't help noticing the third is behaving very differently.

She's a pretty girl, the same age or perhaps a little younger than myself, and 'penitent' is definitely not a word I would use to describe her. She has a constant gleam in her eye and seems to spend the whole day flirting with the men, walking with a different one almost every hour. It may be wrong for me of all people to say it, but I really don't think there can be much doubt as to the type of sin she's having to atone for!

I keep one eye on her to pass the time. And it is certainly interesting to watch the things she gets up to. She seems to go out of her way to flaunt herself and one time, when she thought no one was looking, I actually saw her slyly push her hand down the front of one of the men's trousers. She grasped his penis and quickly tossed him to such an erection that for a long time afterwards he couldn't do anything more than hobble along!

* * *

When we finally arrive at the rest house, I'm so exhausted I only manage half of the supper that's offered to us before the need for sleep overtakes me. I soon discover our accommodation for the night is actually nothing more than a rough barn, strewn with a thick layer of clean straw. There is a wooden barrier halfway down that divides the space into a men's and a women's end, but in our own area we're free to gather up the straw and fashion our own 'beds' wherever we choose.

Still wanting to be alone, I pick a quiet spot in a far corner. After a few minutes' work I have a mattress of sorts prepared and, spreading my travelling cloak beneath me, I settle down and close my eyes.

As I doze off I'm vaguely aware of the others coming in. Without taking much notice, it registers that the two quiet women lay themselves down near the door whilst the young girl, whose name I have learnt is Juliet, makes her bed on the other side of me, at the very back of the barn. I think nothing more about it until much later that night when my sleep is disturbed by strange noises coming from the same area that Juliet is sleeping in.

At first I try to ignore them, but then curiosity gets the better of me. Without making a sound I cautiously part the pile of straw that is separating us – only to reveal Juliet lying in there with one of the pilgrim men on top of her!

For a while they stay just like that, sighing faintly as they pet each other. All the time the man is working Juliet's skirts up higher and higher until they're bunched up round her waist and her smooth thighs are exposed, glowing milky-white in the faint moonlight. She starts to make more noise as the man begins to explore her with his fingers.

The Pleasure Ring

Now, he has one hand on the fastening of his britches, working it free and sliding his pants down ready to go into her. He arches above her, lifting himself up for entry. But then, at the very last moment, I hear her protest, 'No! No! You mustn't! Not without a seed-catcher. You mustn't do it bare!'

The man's exasperation is plain to hear. He hisses back at her, 'I haven't got one. I never thought I'd need one on a pilgrimage, did I?'

There's a tense pause and then Juliet twists away from underneath him and whispers, 'Well then, we'll just have to make do like this instead, won't we?'

With that she turns over away from him and starts working herself backwards against his groin. But as she slides back she lifts her top leg and then lowers it again after she's trapped his cock between the soft, wet flesh of her inner thighs. She tells him to start moving, to push himself backwards and forwards through her legs. It's not what the man really wanted, but it's still good. He starts to get more excited, thrusting harder and harder, making his shaft poke through her thighs further and further until the red head of it bursts out of her crotch every time.

Now, Juliet is masturbating herself with her right hand and reaching to circle the end of his shaft with the fingers of her left. She starts to moan ecstatically. 'Oh God! I've never done anything like this before. I've always wanted to know what it feels like to have a prick. And now I've got one I'm going to wank it hard! I'm going to wank my cock until it shoots spunk everywhere!'

She grips her thighs together so that the man can't pull back and then begins to toss the short stub of penis standing out of her; doing it so fiercely I hear the man groaning with the sensation of it. I watch her writhing around in the straw, furiously beating one hand up and down on 'her' raw, red penis, the other in the split of her sex, masturbating as both a man and a woman at the same time.

And then, suddenly, the head of the penis erupts in Juliet's hand and a violent streak of white come jets out of her. She bows backwards in the darkness, looking down at herself, moving so that she can imagine it's her own cock that's really loosing spunk into the straw. She holds the position for as long as she can and then she buckles forward, climaxing deliriously.

Although I've enjoyed the sight of Juliet's arousal, I soon fall asleep again, thinking of it as nothing more than a young girl's experimenting. It's not until the following night that my eyes are opened properly and I realise how much I've underestimated her!

Although there's no intention on my part, that next evening it comes about that, once again, Juliet and I both choose the same secluded corner of the barn we're told to bed down in. Just as on the previous night I fall asleep quickly, only to be woken again in the small hours by movement close by.

Almost knowing what I'm going to find, I lift myself up and look over towards Juliet's mattress. She's there with a man again – but a different one this time!

This one is obviously more daring than the first. He has nearly all Juliet's clothes off and is himself stripped naked. He's sprawled back into the straw, letting Juliet rub at his shaft, and it's all too obvious from the state of his erection that she's been working on him for some time.

From the things he's saying to her it's also clear he's impatient to mount her now. He tries to push her back onto her cloak. I can barely believe my ears when I hear her say,

The Pleasure Ring

'No! No! You mustn't! Not without a seed-catcher. You mustn't do it bare!'

It's all I can do to contain my astonishment as I have to watch the devious little hussy act out her whole well-rehearsed scene again! Just as before she offers herself so that the man can rub himself between her thighs and then begins to masturbate him mercilessly even as she protests, 'I've never done anything like this before. I've always wanted to know what it feels like to have a prick.'

I have to admit, she's very good. If I hadn't seen it with my own eyes I would have sworn it was her first time. She certainly fools the man. He willingly lets her jerk at his foreskin until his spunk spurts and, once again, she's able to look down and orgasm herself to the sight of come fountaining out of her pretend cock.

I can't help wondering just how many times she's played this trick. How many other unsuspecting men she's duped into fulfilling her bizarre sexual fantasy!

The morning afterwards, Juliet falls in with me as we begin our last, long day of walking to reach Poitiers. She stares at me and then, trying to pull a serious frown she says, 'You look tired!'

I cast her a sideways glance. 'Yes, I know. I haven't been sleeping well. The past two nights I've woken up in the middle of the night, imagining I could see the most unbelievable visions!'

She laughs aloud now. 'So you *were* watching! I knew it. Don't worry, I don't mind. It excited me. When you didn't tell on me after the first night I was sure then we must be having to do this awful trip for the same reason. You got caught doing something you shouldn't have, as well, didn't you? You know, out of the four of us women, only that one over there in the grey is making this trip because she wants to. She must be mad! All the rest of us are being forced to do it as a punishment.

'You see the other woman walking with her? Now I know exactly why she's here! It was a huge scandal. I'll tell you all about it if you like. In fact, I promise to tell you why I'm here, if you'll do the same. Is it a deal?'

We fall back a little from the others so we can talk without being overheard and then she begins. 'The woman's name is Anna Cervois. She's trying to hide it from everyone else here, but I know she's actually from a very well-off family. She and her husband live on a huge estate outside Tours, where I come from.

'The story has it that one afternoon the weather was so pleasant that, on the spur of the moment, she decided to go out riding. She arrived at the stables unannounced only to find them strangely deserted. But as she'd gone to all the trouble of getting dressed ready for her ride, she made up her mind to saddle a horse herself.

'She went over to the stable block, but when she opened the door she walked right in on the stable boy servicing one of the local village girls. Their clothes were strewn everywhere and the lad was on his knees, busily exploring with his tongue between the girl's thighs as she perched on the edge of one of the wooden feeding racks.

'Anna was outraged. She grasped the girl by her hair and, even though she was only half dressed, she threw her out into the courtyard and slammed the door shut behind her.

'Now she turned her attention to the stable boy. She was furious that he'd been spending his time fornicating when he should have been hard at work. She hauled him up off his knees and thrust him forward over the hayrack.

The Pleasure Ring

She had her riding crop with her and she made him stand bent over, gripping the frame with his hands as she started to teach him a lesson he'd never forget.

'The thing was, it wasn't until she had him like that and saw how hairy he was that she realised he was actually a good bit older than she'd first imagined – he must have been at least nineteen – and as she began to lay into him she couldn't help noticing the thick, curly bush sprouting between his thighs – and the huge root that was thrusting out of it.

'It was lean and shiny tight in that way that only young men get. And it was getting longer and harder with every stroke of the crop! It had been a long time since she'd seen such a virile erection and she could hardly take her eyes off it.

'There must have been something in the air that afternoon for Anna suddenly felt such a heat in her sex that the next thing she knew she found herself reaching out and grasping his cock in her spare hand. She began to wank him firmly as she whipped him, making him snort and pant with agitation.

'I'm sure her only thought was to bring him off strongly so that she could have the pleasure of seeing how much come his mighty weapon was going to spray into the hayrack. But she had aroused the lad's passion too fiercely.

'All of a sudden he stood up and tore the crop from her hand. He flung her back onto the straw of an empty stall and, before she could do anything, he had his hands up her skirts. She only had a padded *bande* on underneath, just a narrow strip of wadding fixed between her legs to prevent her sex being chafed by the saddle. The stable lad didn't even make an attempt to remove it, he just jerked the pad to one side and entered her.

'As he pressed down into her she started to bite and shout and kick at him, but really she knew she'd brought it all on herself by what she'd done to him.

'Truth be told, she was more aroused than she would have liked to admit. Her protests began to die away as the stable lad eased her legs up, gradually bending her knees back towards her breasts so that he was entering her from behind her thighs and thrusting into her even more deeply. There was no resistance offered now, his cock felt too good inside her. Her body began to move with his as she gave herself up to the sensation of his shaft sinking so far inside her.

'But what a fright she got when the stable door opened again. It was the girl from the village, come to collect her clothes so she could go home!

'And what an expression came over the young girl's face when she discovered the high and mighty lady of the manor lying on her back with her legs up in the air, rutting like a common wanton. The look she gave her just said, "You're no better than me, are you?"

'She was certainly experienced enough to see the state that Anna was in now. She knew what Anna needed and took pity on her. Even as the stable lad was still thrusting himself in and out of her, she reached in and gently unfastened the *bande*. Then she wet two fingers and slipped them into the folds of Anna's tilted-back vulva. She sought out the hardness of her clitoris and began to rub it steadily.

'Anna pleaded with her to stop, but her eyes told a different story. They both knew she could have pushed the girl's fingers away any time she wanted, but her hands never moved. The sensation of being pleasured by the two of them at once was too arousing!

The Pleasure Ring

'There could be no doubt about it now; it was only going to be a matter of time before they made Anna come. She began to call out as she neared crisis, but the vulgar things that came out of her mouth so excited the stable lad it brought on his own orgasm before he could deliver her to her goal.

'At the moment he climaxed, he pulled out of Anna's sex and held himself above her lips. There was a second's pause and then his seed began to shoot out all over her clitoris.

'As soon as he started, the girl changed her fingers to a whisking motion, deliberately whipping his hot come up into a thick lather. The stimulation of having her slippery quim touched like that would have made her orgasm soon enough but, when Anna looked down, she saw what was being done to her. Saw how the girl had beaten the spunk up so hard the whole of her upturned sex was being buried under a creamy white froth of bubbling foam. And the instant she looked, she just came everywhere!'

Juliet's voice is full of amazement. 'The stupid thing was, she was so wracked by guilt that, the very next day, she actually went and confessed everything to her priest. Can you believe that? Girl or no girl, if I'd ever come across a lusty stud like that in my stables I'd have kept very quiet about it and suddenly developed a keen interest in my horses! I'm absolutely sure I would have never admitted anything to anyone.

'I'm only here myself now because I got caught and if I could have got out of this I would have done. Though maybe I can't complain too much. Everything that's happened to me has been my own fault and, if I'm perfectly honest, I've been lucky to get away with just this!

'You see, I'd been having this affair with a man who said he was single, but I found out he was lying. When I discovered he was married I was so cross I decided to go round to his house and make things as uncomfortable for him as I could.

'I waited for an afternoon that I knew he'd be out and then I went up and knocked at his door. I had a travelling trunk with me and when his wife answered the door I spun her a story about being a distant cousin of her husband's. I made up some tale about travelling to an aunt's house in the North and having been stranded in Tours overnight. I said I'd remembered that she and her husband lived in the town and I'd searched them out in the hope that they could offer me a bed until the next day.

'I think that, even then, his wife was a little suspicious, but all the same she invited me in and made me welcome. She showed me to a guest room and left me to wash and clean myself up. I'd made sure I'd arrived looking as though I'd spent the day in a dusty coach.

'All the deception was worth it for the expression on my lover's face when he came home later and found me sitting in his front room, chatting with his wife. I tell you, he went as white as a sheet! I immediately jumped up and ran over to kiss him in welcome and as I put my head close to his I whispered, "I'm your cousin!"

'Under the circumstances I thought he handled it remarkably well. He had to sit down, but it wasn't long before he'd recovered enough to be able to play along with the pretence of exchanging news of imaginary relatives.

'After a half-hour or so his wife announced she had to begin the evening meal and I said I'd take the opportunity to go upstairs and change.

'Just as I knew he would my lover waited a few minutes and then made some excuse to his wife about wanting to come upstairs to check I had everything I needed.

'I knew he was going to be really angry with me. He came thundering into my room, demanding to know exactly what I was up to. But I had an another shock waiting for him! When he burst in I was wearing a dressing gown, but as soon as he started speaking to me I slipped it off my shoulders, revealing myself naked underneath except for a little silk pouch, barely big enough to contain my quim. It was so tight on me it fitted like a second skin, showing every fold and ridge of my mound.

'That really made him panic. He started saying, "For pity's sake, Juliet, put your clothes on. What would my wife say if she found you like this? What is it you want from me?"

'I was very controlled. I just answered coolly, "I want sex. I want you to take me on the floor. Now!"

'He couldn't believe I meant it. "You're crazy. Here in my own house, with my wife downstairs? It's madness! The kitchen's right below us!"

'But I could see his cock getting hard in his pants and I knew he was going to do it. I lay down on the rug in front of him and tugged the straining ties of the pouch loose; letting my wet sex burst free of its silky prison. I must have looked quite a sight as I lay there with my knees bent up and my glistening quim slowly flowering open as it swelled out from captivity.

'His pants were down by the time he reached me. He fell between my legs and sank right into me. It was wonderful. Hot and fast and urgent. I had carpet burns on my back for days afterwards. My little arse was bouncing up and down on the floor like a ball. We'd only been at it a few minutes when we heard his wife calling to him from downstairs. He tried to get up but I held him down tightly, biting at his ear, moaning, "Not until you make me come!"

'That really spurred him on. He started to go faster and faster. His wife *must* have been able to hear us now. She called up again, really suspicious this time, "What's going on? What are you two doing up there?" I heard her beginning to climb the stairs. He tried to pull away again, but I was too close to let him go. I knew it was only going to take a few more thrusts to bring me to the most incredible climax.

'It was a race against time; he started to pound into me like a madman. I could hear her tread on the stairs, getting closer and closer. I was so near. I kept saying, "Don't stop! Don't stop!" But she was only seconds away and he was getting desperate now. He was almost begging me. "Come on! Come on! Come now!" There were only moments left. She was on the landing. Outside my room!

'Then the door handle turned and she came flying in. And there I was – sitting on the edge of the bed in my dressing gown, calmly combing my hair!

'She was so taken aback, she could hardly speak. The poor woman had been so sure of what she'd heard, but now it all seemed completely foolish. She started to mumble, "I'm sorry, so sorry! I thought . . . thought I heard . . . No, it doesn't matter. I'm sorry, I was looking for my husband."

'She turned to go and we nearly got away with it, but just at that moment there was a stifled moan from behind the door. She stepped back and swung it closed and there was her husband, standing with his pants round his ankles.

'He hadn't come with me, but he'd gone too far. All the time he'd been hiding behind the door his cock had been stiffening and tightening, the orgasm building up inside him until he'd lost control and it had started to pump out

The Pleasure Ring

of him of its own accord. His hands were clasped over his crotch now, but it was no use. He was still spilling and, try as he might to hide it, the hot, sticky spunk was leaking out between his fingers and oozing down the outside of his hands.

'You would have thought his wife would have been more angry with him than me, but that wasn't the case at all. She wouldn't hear a word against him. As far as she was concerned he was totally innocent and I'd schemed to seduce him.

'It was unfortunate for me she was not only very religious, but also a good friend of the local priest. She wanted him to have me sentenced to the usual punishment for a convicted seductress – to be taken to the town square and publicly padlocked into an iron chastity belt for a year and a day.

'That would have driven me mad! It was lucky for me that my father intervened and used his influence, and a very large donation to the Church, to get my sentence reduced to walking this pilgrimage.'

I know it's my turn to confess my misdeeds now. But, although I'm sure Juliet would be more than interested to hear the true story of why I'm here, I can't help feeling a little caution is called for. There can be no useful purpose in revealing the intimate details of my wanton past to her. Much better that I cast myself in a better light by making myself out to be the victim of a terrible injustice.

I decide to tell her a different tale, to pass off as my own experience an incident from one of those erotic novels I used to steal from the servant girls. One that has often come to my mind at night-times!

I set the tone by starting off meekly. 'I really do think you've formed the wrong impression of me. I'm here not because of my own wrongdoings, but because of another's lies.

'Last year I got married and went to live in Angers with my new husband. He is quite high up in society there and upon my arrival I was introduced to all the important people of the town. I was keen to fit in and, as I play the harpsichord a little, I soon found myself in demand to provide entertainment at all sorts of parties and musical evenings.

'Just before Christmas, it snowed really hard for the first time since I'd arrived in Angers. Everywhere was covered in drifts, feet deep in places. But it so happened that I'd been asked to play at the mayor's house that same afternoon. Although the journey across town was going to be difficult, I knew a great many people would still be expecting me there and I didn't want to disappoint them.

'I set out in my carriage, but we only managed to get halfway before we found our way down the streets blocked by the snow. It had begun to come down thickly again and I was worried the horses were going to become trapped in the drifts. I decided to send the coachman back with the carriage and carry on by myself, on foot.

'This wasn't as rash as it sounds because I thought I knew a short cut to the mayor's house. I'd often noticed an alleyway that looked as though it led almost directly there. Being sheltered, it was a lot clearer of snow and I truly believed I would be safely there in no more than a couple of minutes.

'I turned off the street into the quiet passage, soon leaving the few other people that were out and about far behind me. The lane was much narrower and more out-of-the-way than I'd imagined. I'm sure normally I would have turned back straight away, but on that day everywhere looked so

The Pleasure Ring

much more unthreatening and friendly covered in pure white snow.

'A long, high, windowless wall ran all the way down one side of the winding alley, but it was only when I rounded a corner and came across an archway closed off by sturdy iron bars that I realised I was actually travelling along the outside wall of the town prison.

'The archway must have originally been some kind of back entrance, but now newer buildings had been erected in front of it and shielded it from the rest of the building. It was an ideal place to hide away unseen and, indeed, there was a lone inmate standing under its cover doing just that.

'As I approached he turned to look at me. I was a little nervous, but carried on walking. As I drew level he called out, "Madam, madam, please will you help me? Look there on the ground in front of you! My money pouch. I dropped it through the bars and I can't reach it. Please, I beg you, pass it back to me. It is all the money I have in the world."

'When I looked down, I saw a brown leather pouch lying on the snow. It seemed churlish to walk past and ignore such a simple request, so I paused for a second and bent down to retrieve it for him.

'Not wanting to go too close to the bars, I tossed it over to him, but his fingers were so cold he wasn't nimble enough to catch it and it dropped to the ground once more.

'Without thinking, I stepped forward to pick it up again and in that instant he had me! He suddenly flicked one end of a long leather belt out round my waist and then caught it as it wrapped round me. Quickly pulling it through the next bar, he buckled it tight so that my back was hauled up tight against the two poles.

'I cried out for help, but the man just laughed and said, "Shout out all you like, there's nobody to hear you!"

'Working behind me, he jerked my woollen cape off my shoulders. As soon as it was pulled away he put his hands inside the collar of my blouse and ripped the front open from top to bottom, shooting all the buttons off into the snow.

'Moments later I felt the blade of a knife slide up the lacing at the back of my bustier. As he cut it loose my hands instinctively came up to clasp it to me and keep my breasts covered. But folding my arms across my chest just made it all the easier for him to slip the blade down the waistband of my skirt unhindered. He sliced that open as well and it fell to the ground in a drape of cloth, revealing my loose knickers underneath.

'I could hear his breathing getting heavier. I let the bustier go and made a grab for his hands, but I was too late. His fingers had already wormed their way inside the topband and it only took one strong tug to split the seams apart and leave me naked. The sensation of the ice-cold iron bars pressing against my exposed buttocks made me gasp for breath.

'He called out behind me and moments later there was the sound of footsteps coming under the archway – the sound of other men arriving. Grimy hands began pushing through the bars, groping at my breasts and bottom. It made it worse that I couldn't twist round far enough to see any of them. They were just hands and voices – and cocks.

'Right from the start, I knew what was going to happen to me. The man who had tricked me was the first. The way I was pulled back against those two bars left a gap in the middle just at the right place for him. My sex

The Pleasure Ring

was practically presented through the bars for him to go into.

'He drew himself close in behind me and hissed, "I'm going to make your cunny very cold and then I'm going to make it very hot!" He bent down and scooped up a handful of snow and I heard myself scream as he ground it up into my vulva. It was so cold! So unbelievably icy it hurt. It's hard to admit, but it was almost a relief when he pushed forward and sank his red-hot prick into me.

'He started to rod me through the bars. It was snowing again now. Flakes started to settle on my breasts. My nipples were blue with cold. Incredibly hard and swollen, but bright blue.

'He was thrusting into me deeply, banging his hips against the bars. I kept struggling as hard as I could, but there was nothing I could do to stop him poking his cock through and entering me. Men were arriving all the time now. He laughed. "You're in for a real shagging, lady. Some of these men haven't had a woman in six months. Best I grease you well for them now!"

'He grunted loudly and I felt his spunk shooting into me. Almost before he'd finished he was jostled away and another man pushed forward to mount me.

'And then, as soon as he'd come inside me, that man was pulled away and yet another one immediately took his place. It just went on and on like that. It wasn't long before I totally exhausted myself trying to wrestle free. In the end I just hung forward limply against the belt round my waist and let them take me. I couldn't see any of the men's faces, couldn't feel anything but their rough hands on my breasts and their slimy cocks going into me. I lost count of the number of pricks I had to take. There were big ones and small ones, thin ones and thick ones. A couple that were absolutely huge; great monsters that pushed right through the bars and jammed up deep inside me.

'Every so often a man would shout out, "Her cunny's overheating!" and another handful of snow would be pushed into me to cool me down.

'The really awful thing was they were absolutely right. The friction of the continuous cocking they were giving me was the only thing that was keeping me warm. Every other part of my body was blue with cold, but my sex was glowing red.

'I must have stayed like that for an hour or more. Can you imagine that! A solid hour of shafting and spurting orgasms. When I looked down now there was a great milky pool of frozen spunk on the ground between my legs.

'I kept thinking of how all the mayor's guests would be looking at the clock and wondering where I'd got to. They'd be tut-tutting over my lateness; having no idea that the reason I wasn't there playing music for them was that I was bent over, bound naked in the snow, being continuously used from behind by a never-ending queue of sex-starved criminals.

'My release only came when one of the prisoners heard someone coming down the alleyway and they all scattered. The belt was hurriedly unbuckled and the moment I was set free my legs folded under me. I was so weak I just slumped down into the snow, but as the footsteps rounded the corner I was never so glad to hear another human being approaching!

'That was, until I looked up to see my rescuer and found the face of the local priest scowling down at me.

'Of all the people in Angers, it would have to be him that discovered me like this! The man had borne a grudge against my husband for years and now I'd presented him

The Pleasure Ring

with an ideal opportunity to get even. He brushed aside my truthful explanation and insisted instead that he'd caught me in the act of whoring. The next Sunday he denounced me from the pulpit in front of all the town and through no sin of my own I was sentenced by the church elders to complete this pilgrimage.'

By the time my story's finished, Juliet's eyes are twinkling with excitement. She sighs breathlessly. 'Oohh! I'm sure you never meant it to, but all your talk about being shagged by dozens of cocks has made me so horny I can't bear it. There won't be any chance when we get to the Abbey tonight, so I'm going to have to do something about it now!' As she hurries away up the path she calls back, 'You can watch again if you like!'

She quickly catches up with the man whom I recognise as her visitor from the first night. She whispers something in his ear and then quietly drifts off into the woods beside the pathway. The man holds back until he's sure her departure has gone unnoticed and then he slips away as well.

Creeping after them would be too much; I've already decided not to do that. But, by chance, the place they've stolen off to is on the other side of a low hill that runs alongside the pilgrims' way. There's a narrow track that slopes off from the main path up to the summit and, by doing no more than following that track, I'm soon able to observe them over the edge of the ridge.

Looking down the other side, I see Juliet weaving her way through the trees some distance ahead of the man. She's walking along with her skirts lifted right up over her hips, exposing the full rounds of her delightful bare arse to him as she goes. She's really leading him on, stopping every so often and glancing back over her shoulder at him in the most provocative way. It isn't long before the man begins to speed up, feverishly unbuttoning his britches as he runs along. He soon has his cock out in his hands, rubbing it jerkily as he lopes after her.

He catches up with her in a little clearing. In one movement he grabs her and spears himself into her sex from behind. Half carrying, half pushing her, he guides her awkwardly over to a fallen tree at the edge of the clearing, still thrusting into her vigorously all the way across the open grass. Flinging her forward over the damp, mossy log he tugs her dresses up over her head and off.

She looks beautiful in the morning sunshine. Her curving, young girl's body exposed as nature intended in the midst of the wild forest. Her smooth, pale skin set against the dark, moist greenery of the glade.

You can imagine how annoyed I am when I notice I've been spotted by some of the other pilgrims on the path below and I realise I have to leave before seeing the end of their mating!

Chapter 8

By sunset on this third day we come in sight of the Abbey walls and – hungry, tired and footsore – we finally pass through its massive arched gates. We make our way to the lodging house, just one of the many stone buildings standing jostled together round a huge courtyard in front of the Abbey itself.

There are a great many other pilgrims at the lodging house. We're all fed our supper together in the common dining hall and then after prayers we're shown to our resting place for the night. Mine, like all the others, is a simple stone cell in a long corridor of exactly similar rooms, each furnished with just a straw mattress on a wooden frame, a wall shelf and a candle holder.

Whilst the others are preparing for bed, I seek out the host monk and give him the note, telling him the Abbot wished it to be delivered to him as soon as I arrived. He is most surprised at this, but promises to have it delivered to his master immediately.

All the other pilgrims have retired by the time I return and I start undressing quickly, wanting to get to bed before the short stub of candle I've been given burns out. It's whilst I'm doing this that I notice the flickering light of another candle approaching along the corridor. It stops outside my cell and there's a single, light knock at the door.

I open it to find before me a monk dressed in a short black habit, his hood pulled fully forward, hiding his face from the light. He informs me curtly that the Abbot has ordered that I am to be moved to spend the night in the special guest's quarters. I must gather up my things and follow him straight away.

I bundle my few possessions together and go with him. He leads me along hurriedly, hardly giving me time to catch my breath. We never meet another soul, passing through the labyrinth of the darkened building like ghosts. I follow him in silence along corridor after corridor, up and down stairway after winding stairway, through doorway after doorway until, at long last, he turns into a dusty passage and, unlocking the end door with a great iron key, he gestures for me to go in.

This room is very different from my bare cell. There are hangings on the wall, matting on the floor, a clothes chest, a water bowl and, best of all, a real wooden bed with a proper mattress and linen sheets.

With his head turned down, the monk lights a candle in a holder and mutters a few words of parting from the depths of his habit. Suddenly overcome with tiredness from my days of journeying, I wearily strip off my clothes and slip between the crisp, fresh sheets with a grateful sigh. I blow the candle out and fall asleep as soon as my head meets the pillow.

By my reckoning it's some time just after midnight that I'm startled awake by a strange noise in the room. I can hear something creaking, something exactly like the sound of heavy, wooden machinery turning slowly; cogs and levers

The Pleasure Ring

grinding together. Rigid with fear, I peer into the blackness around me, but the room's so dark I can't see a thing. The only thing I do know is that the noise is coming from very close by – from somewhere directly beneath the bed!

It's only when I feel the first movement that, too late, I realise what it is. The bedframe is splitting in two! The mattress is pulling apart from head to foot to open up a gap right down the middle!

The machinery is moving faster now. I'm starting to slip down into a yawning black chasm. I try to get a grip on the sheets to claw myself back up, but they just pull in with me. My legs drop down and I disappear after them, falling through the split, dropping naked out of the sheets through a hole in the floor and onto a steep wooden chute. I start to slide down it, slithering out of control through the total darkness, twisting and spiralling faster and faster.

I hurtle on and on until, after what seems like hours, I tumble out of the end of the chute and land heavily on a thick pile of soft red cushions. As I look around me, my only thought is that I've been taken down to Hell. I'm in some sort of underground chamber, the stone walls lit by the licking flames of wall torches. There's nothing in the chamber except for one single, thick wooden stake standing out of the floor in the centre of the room, surrounded by more of the cushions. It's very hot. Maybe it's just the heat from the torches but, all the same, it makes me feel uneasy. I try to tell myself that this is only a bad dream. But, if it really is a nightmare, it's only just beginning!

Before I've had time to gather my senses, strong hands grab me and drag me over to the stake. My wrists are pulled together sharply and my hands are bound to the post with a length of strong rope. I'm left kneeling on all fours on the cushions with my hands tied uncomfortably above my head.

I twist my head round as far as I can, wanting to confront my captor. But the figure I see sends a shudder down my spine.

It's the black monk! The same one that led me to the room.

As he stands watching me impassively, he slowly pulls his cowl back. But, terrifyingly, it's only to reveal that now his features are hidden by a tight leather mask that fits his head like a hangman's hood. Only the dark coals of his eyes peer out at me through narrow slits.

I start to shout at him in an anger born of fear; ordering him to set me free, demanding to know why I've been bound like this. His only answer is to come closer and begin forcing more of the cushions under me, building them up under my belly until my bare arse is held pushed out behind me. All the time I'm ranting at him, cursing him, but he ignores me completely, silently finishing his task and then moving away out of sight into the shadows behind me.

He's only gone for a few moments and when he returns I blanch to see the thing he's holding in his hand. It's a tawse; a half-dozen supple birch saplings bound together into an evil instrument of punishment.

I start to scream, but my wails just ring back off the stone walls, mocking me. Who would ever hear such futile cries for help from this secret room; this hidden place buried so deep beneath the Abbey cellars that no one else even knows it exists?

The black monk takes his position beside me and lifts the tawse high above his head. I have no idea who he is or why he's brought me here, but I know now exactly what he's going to do to me.

The Pleasure Ring

His arm scythes through the air and he brings the birch down hard across my buttocks, catching me across both rounded cheeks, making me gasp with shock as the stinging pain courses through me.

He waits now, deliberately holding back until the tingling sharpness of that first savage stroke has faded away. Then I hear the tawse cutting through the air again and another stroke comes. Then another and another. There is no end to it. I cry out in agony, but he whips me on and on, caning me as hard as he can.

Though I can hardly bear it I have to turn my head to watch the strokes coming. And when I look I'm appalled by what I see.

He's beating me so furiously that every time he raises his arm he makes the edge of his short habit jerk upwards to reveal his hugely stiff prick standing, bare, beneath it!

His erection is enormous and obscenely bizarre. The purple shaft of it is grossly distorted, curving upwards along its whole length like the sprouting root of some vile plant. I can clearly see how every stroke of the birch makes the rough material rasp over its straining head, bringing the monk to even greater arousal.

My buttocks are on fire now. I plead for mercy, beg him to stop, but he takes no notice. He just keeps raining lashes down on me, thrashing the tawse across my arse in a sexual frenzy.

The minutes that follow become a blur. The only thing I can remember is his hand rising and falling over and over again. That and a ring on his finger, a plain gold band with a single ruby set in it. Each and every time he lifts his arm that dark red stone flashes for a moment in the torchlight. My eyes fix on it, knowing that the sight of its fire is nothing less than an awful warning that another stroke is about to follow.

I think I'm going to faint. I cling desperately to the stake as I feel myself swooning away. But, just as I fall forwards, the monk's strength gives out at last and he lets the tawse drop to the ground beside him, chest heaving, struggling for breath.

If my eyes brim with tears of relief, they are too soon in coming. He's not finished with me yet, for now I see him grasp his habit and feverishly tug it off over his masked head. His body is glistening with sweat underneath. The end of his cock is like a polished ball balanced on the end of a bent stick. It's shiny wet, disgustingly lubricated with his own excitement.

He lurches over to me, legs split apart as though his prick is a heavy weight hanging between his thighs. I beg for him to spare me, but I'm helpless to stop him. He straddles himself across my raised hips and slides the whole length of his iron-hard, curved shaft into my unguarded mound like a cutlass being thrust into its scabbard.

He starts driving into me ferociously, stabbing his cock into my sex from tip to hilt, slapping his thighs against my smarting, tortured buttocks. His hands come round my waist, lifting me up, pulling me back onto him even further. He's going so very deep inside me, filling me to the very limit with his great arc of flesh.

Now it is his turn to cry out. He bellows like a bull, unable to move again. I feel his legs stiffen, his thighs clench. His cock stays jammed inside me but moves of its own accord, beyond his control now. And, the way it is with men when they come with this much lust, I feel him start to pulse inside me long before he begins to spend. His shaft begins to throb sickeningly, jolting up and down,

The Pleasure Ring

rehearsing the action of pumping seed. Once, twice, three times he jerks dry and nothing comes. Then he screams in agony as the spunk begins to spit out of his over-engorged cock with the searing pain of boiling hot vinegar.

When it's finally over, he pulls out of me slowly and staggers away, exhausted. He takes a tiny bottle from a niche in the wall and, uncorking it, he pulls my head back and holds the bottle to my lips, forcing me to swallow some of the bitter cordial inside. Seconds later the room seems to start spinning. I feel myself slipping away, drifting off into darkness . . .

When I come to, it's like a mist rising from in front of my eyes. I sit bolt upright, gripped by terror.

But it's alright. There's sunlight on me. It's morning. I'm not in the chamber anymore.

The strangest thing is that I'm not in the special guest room either. I'm back in my stone cell, back on the straw mattress.

I've been woken by the door opening. The host monk is standing there calling to me that the Abbot wants to see me straight away.

Stunned speechless from the horrors of the night, I dress quickly and go with him out of the lodging house and across the grass courtyard to the Abbot's private quarters. I'm shown into his library to find him writing at his desk, my note of absolution to one side of him. He waves me to take a seat, but I can't contain myself any longer and, to his great astonishment, I begin to pour out the whole story of the terrible ordeal I've been through.

He listens patiently and then summons me to follow him back to the lodging house, calling the host monk to attend so that I can repeat my story in front of him.

The monk is baffled. He assures me no message was sent from the Abbot last night about my sleeping arrangements. No man he knows fits the description of the black monk who I claim had imprisoned me and, furthermore, he reminds me that it is grey, not black habits that the monks of the Abbey wear.

When I insist, the Abbot allows me the chance to show them the room with the opening bed that I had been taken to. But the old building is like a maze and everything looks so different in the daylight. Even though I hunt throughout the lodgings, I'm unable to remember any of the twisting, turning route I had been led along.

After an hour of fruitless searching the Abbot tells me, a little tetchily, that I have taken up enough of his time and that we must return to his rooms.

Once we're alone again, he rounds on me and tells me firmly that, in his opinion, all the things I have convinced myself I'd experienced were, in fact, no more than a vivid dream brought about by my own guilty conscience. I begin to realise that he doesn't believe a word of what I've said. It's only then that I remember I really do have proof that I'm not making it all up.

I say to him angrily, 'If you don't think I'm telling the truth, then how do you explain this?'

I turn away from him and hitch up my skirt just enough to expose the lower part of my angry, red buttocks. I hear him let out a gasp as he sees what I look like.

He comes to my side and gently persuades me to lift my skirt up higher to let him see the full extent of the marks on me. He insists I let him put some soothing ointment on the livid weals that cover my inflamed cheeks and immediately goes to fetch the cream and a pad of

The Pleasure Ring

cloth. His concern overcomes my embarrassment and I reluctantly allow myself to be leaned forward over the back of a chair so that he can apply the lotion. I can see my whole arse is crisscrossed with thin crimson stripes, raised into a hundred painful ridges. I flinch again and again as he dabs the cold cream onto me.

As he's working away he tells me he has no doubts now that I have been terribly chastised, caned by a fiend who has obviously taken evil pleasure in administering every vicious stroke. But the only explanation must be that I have been visited by a divine messenger sent from Above – a spirit sent down to Earth to administer the punishment that the Almighty had judged was the true and proper penitence for my immoral sins.

As he finishes and lets my skirts drop again, he tells me that, in view of these miraculous events, he has decided that I have suffered enough. He will sign my note of absolution without delay so that I may return home today with his blessing.

I turn round to thank him properly, to take his offered hand and kiss it gratefully.

It's then that I see the ring on his finger. A single red ruby, set in gold!

The truth hits me like a thunderbolt. It was no spirit, no divine messenger that wielded that tawse over me last night. It was the Abbot!

I realise now that all the time he's been tenderly salving my buttocks it is his own handiwork he's been examining! And arousing himself at the sight of what he's done to me, too, I'll wager!

I'm so outraged I act without thinking. I thrust my hand forward and snatch his heavy robes up.

I've made no mistake. The evidence is there standing

hard and rolled back. That same enormous, curved erection, just as red and swollen with excitement as the last time we met!

In a fit of temper I slap his shaft as hard as I can. I smack it loudly with the flat of my hand only to make it spring to the side and then bounce back all the stiffer. The Abbot winces in pain and then smiles as he pulls his robe down over his smarting pole. 'You've been very clever to uncover my little deception, Amande. But I'm afraid you've been very foolish as well. You should have waited a while. Have you forgotten I haven't signed your note yet?

'You know, of course, that until that's done it's quite within my power to have you taken out into the courtyard and flogged until sunset as your penitence. How would you like that?'

He looks at me questioningly and sees the fear on my face.

'Don't look so worried. The sole reason I arranged to have you sent here to Poitiers was so that I could take pleasure with you myself. Now, your discovery has finally given me the opportunity to fulfil one of my most shameful fantasies. I promise you that I will sign your note and release you when you have performed this act with me, but you must come with me quickly now. We don't have much time!'

He takes my arm and hustles me through a side door. We hurry along a covered passage and down some narrow stairs to stop in front of a curtained archway.

He holds me back and goes through it alone. A moment later he returns and hoarsely orders me to take off all my clothes.

As soon as I'm naked he ushers me through the curtain. I'm shocked to find that we emerge from behind a massive

The Pleasure Ring

stone pillar into the echoing quiet of the great Abbey itself. We're in the nave, right in the middle of the choir stalls.

The Abbot pulls me over to his lectern, the huge desk where he stands during services. It's set at one end of the stalls, higher up than all the other seats. It's big wooden framed box, panelled in with solid oak on three sides.

Urging me to hurry, he forces me to kneel down and crawl inside the lectern so that he can move in behind me and hastily arrange his robe to cover me from sight.

Just as he finishes a bell begins to toll solemnly. There's a tiny split in the front of the oak panelling. I peer through it to see lines of monks beginning to file into the Abbey down the long aisle.

The Abbot is so aroused he can't wait any longer. Even before the first monk has taken his seat I feel him gathering the front of his robe up, baring his cock. His hands cup my buttocks, pulling me open so he can furtively slide himself right into me with only the slightest change of position.

The monks begin their chanting and he starts moving very slowly. It's plain to me now what his intention is – he's going to take me like this all through the mass, secretly inching his cock in and out of my sex even as he stands there with his hands joined together in prayer.

There's so much danger. There are monks sitting just a few feet away from us. The absolute wickedness of what we're doing begins to excite me. I start to touch myself.

The Abbot senses what I'm doing and he tries to stop me by reaching down and squeezing my poor, birched cheeks in his hands. I have to bite my lip to keep from calling out, but I'm so ready now that even the stinging pain just arouses me further.

It's so hot and cramped and awkward here inside the darkness of the box. I'm all bent up. I have to support my weight on one hand and masturbate with the other. I really want to rub my clit, but I can't because I know I'm so wet it'll make all sorts of noise. I just have to do it with my whole hand, soundlessly rolling my nub back and forth under my palm, bringing the pleasure on crudely like that. I start to buck and heave, struggling to keep silent as the climax rises inside me.

And then it happens so quickly it takes me by surprise. I jerk back onto the Abbot's prick and hang there, impaled limply, head lolling forward, coming off in the most unholy, sinful way I could ever imagine.

Chapter 9

My blasphemous behaviour upsets the Abbot's plans a little. Almost as soon as I've come off he follows after me, having to grip the lectern to support himself as his hips pump and he spends into me silently.

It seems a long time after that before the service ends and we can steal away back to his rooms. Once we're there he does sign my note as promised, but he doesn't let me leave the Abbey straight away. He's no fool. He has me locked away in strict solitary confinement for a week. Partly to make it look to everyone as though I have been sentenced to a proper penitence, but mostly to ensure that all evidence of the lustful whipping he gave me has had time to fade away.

The days seem to drag by as slowly as any I've ever known. You can imagine the joy I feel when the eighth morning finally comes round and a monk comes to release me and escort me from the Abbey.

If I'm happy at that moment it doesn't last long. As I go out of the gates, I hear my name being called coldly. My heart sinks to see my husband's sister opening the door of a carriage and beckoning me in. I've only met this woman once before, at my wedding feast, but I know her to be a thin, dry old spinster of little humour, a fanatically religious woman who is able to see the seeds of sin in almost every pleasurable activity. In my mind I always refer to her as The Stick.

With little enthusiasm for our meeting, I climb into her carriage, thinking only that Charles has sent her here to collect me. But, when I go to sit down, I see the seats are piled high with my bags and belongings. I turn to The Stick for some explanation and in response she hands me a letter from Charles.

In it he tells me that the scandal I have caused has made it impossible for him to continue living in Angers. The only course open to him has been to shut the house up and go to live with relatives in Paris. It is unthinkable that I should join him there so, for the foreseeable future, he has decided that I shall live with his sister. He is placing me under her strict control and guidance in the hope that she will be able to cast the wantonness out of me.

He has added a chilling footnote. He makes it clear that, should I not submit absolutely to his sister's wishes, the Abbot of Poitiers has assured him that he is more than willing to have me returned here and placed, forcibly if necessary, under his direct control.

I shudder to think of the many ways that the Abbot could enjoy exerting his 'control' over me. I have no choice but to do exactly as Charles wishes – from now on I'm going to have to do every single thing The Stick tells me to.

As she orders the carriage to drive on, a vision suddenly comes into my head. I see Angel pointing at me and laughing, gloating at the havoc she's brought down on me. And when I think of that I feel a burning rage inside me. I turn angrily to search through the few possessions that Charles has allowed me to take away with me. I pretend to be sorting through them, seeing what is there, but really I'm looking for one thing only.

The Pleasure Ring

I finally discover my jewellery box tucked away in the very bottom of one of the bags. I don't bring it out though. I open it hidden away in there, sliding my hand into it like a thief. I explore the contents with my fingertips until, at last, they touch upon the thing I've been searching so hard for – the gold circle of the pleasure ring.

I take hold of it and slide it gently onto the little finger of my right hand; the same finger I first tried it on, so naively, that time in Paris all those months ago. From this day onwards I will wear the ring on that finger as a reminder of the vow I make now.

For I swear with all my heart that, someday, somehow, I will take my revenge on the woman who has destroyed my life, the woman I hate more than anyone else in the world.

That bitch, Angel.

Chapter 10

The next three months are the worst I've ever known.

The Stick lives in a draughty, grey house far away from the nearest town. I never see anyone or do anything. She goes out of her way to make my life a misery. The days slip by in an endless round of church meetings and listening to long passages from uplifting religious tracts being read to me. In the evening we sit together in the parlour and sew Christian mottoes on samplers.

She never leaves me alone for a minute. I have to accompany her everywhere. Even at nights she sleeps in a boxroom off from my bedroom, keeping the adjoining door open so that she can watch me. She makes sure she lies awake until I've gone to sleep, determined that I will never even get a chance to masturbate whilst I'm in her charge.

Day and night I have to wear a pair of drawers she's had sewn up specially for me. They're made of thick, padded cotton with the crotch corseted with whalebone in such a way that it bulges out over my sex. The high waistband laces up complicatedly at the back so that I can't undo it myself. Once she's tied them on me the drawers are like a chastity belt, locking my itching-to-be-rubbed sex away out of reach. There's absolutely no way I can even get near to squirming my fingers in and touching myself. Though, God knows, I've tried often enough!

Going without coming is driving me crazy. I haven't orgasmed in weeks now. I'm almost beginning to think it's worth getting myself sent back to the Abbot. At least I know he'd be more than glad to let me climax for him.

The sexual tension keeps building inside me day after day, until it gets so I think I'm going to burst. I'm so frustrated I just know something has to happen.

And when it finally does it's at the only time The Stick can't get at me.

I start to orgasm in my sleep!

It's brought on by a special dream, a powerful erotic fantasy that keeps coming to me again and again. Always the same, and always too exciting to bear...

I'm at a grand ball. It's very formal, all the men are dressed in black frock coats, the women in ball gowns. I'm wearing the jacket with the floor-length hooped skirt that Angel made me buy for that night at the opera. All around me happy couples are dancing and waltzing, but The Stick is here in charge of me and she won't allow me to join in.

She's made me come to the ball wearing the chastity drawers under my skirt, but that hasn't stopped me feeling horny. Even though I'm standing at the side of the dance floor trying to look innocent, I'm practically fainting with the need to orgasm. I can't think about anything else.

Suddenly, I feel a movement under my skirts. It's part of the fantasy that I realise exactly what's happening without even looking down. I know that a small, secret trap door has been opened up in the wooden floor under my skirt, just in front of my feet, and that someone has climbed up from out of the hole to crouch inside the arched tent of the

The Pleasure Ring

material. It's a man but he's very small – a dwarf. I know full well I only have to call out and he'll be discovered, but I want to come so badly I don't say a word.

There's the faintest noise of metal clanging together as the dwarf assembles a bizarre ironwork stand between my legs. The main part of it is a strong pole that he fits into a socket in the dance floor that, somehow, no one has ever noticed before. The top of the pole has a head fitted on it shaped into a wide W, just like a devil's fork. Only, in the middle peak, there's another piece added – a hard, curved pad sitting at right angles to the prongs.

I feel the dwarf reaching up and sliding one side of a pair of scissors into the crotch of my drawers. I hardly dare to breathe as the cold, sharp steel blades begin to snip through the padding and boning so very close to the vulnerable folds of my labia. Next goes the laced-up waistband and then the tattered remnants fall down my legs to lie at my feet, exposing my sex completely. I know The Stick is going to be furious with me when she finds what I've let the dwarf do to the drawers. But there's no point in stopping him now, I'm already too deeply in trouble.

Now the dwarf guides the W of the pole up from behind me so that the cheeks of my buttocks are resting into both cups. With the prongs like that, the curved pad in the middle presses right up into my crotch, following round the shape of it except where the two ends turn up sharply to probe into me more severely.

Soon, there's a different sound. The dwarf is turning some kind of geared machinery on the side of the pole that's making the head part inch upwards. I feel it pushing up under my buttocks, rising higher and higher until my feet are lifted just off the floor and I find myself balanced precariously in mid-air.

Taking advantage of my unstable position, the dwarf quickly grasps one of my legs and folds it upwards so that my knee is bent outwards. There's a short rod sticking out either side of the pole just below the prongs. He places the sole of my foot onto the rod and then fastens it there with a short loop of cord tied round my ankle. When he brings the other foot up as well I'm left squatting on the top of the pole with my knees spread disgustingly wide open and all my weight bearing down on the cups of the prongs.

The incredible excitement of this part of the fantasy is the uncomfortable 'nastiness' of sitting like this. The way the thin metal bar of the prongs is embedding itself into the tender flesh right across the bottom of my buttocks. The way the hard pad is like a tiny saddle. The turned-up prow ends sticking into me like horns, one at the front, one at the rear. As I sway backwards and forwards trying to get my balance they work themselves deeper and deeper into my sex and arse, until they're pushed in so far the whole saddle is almost lost inside me.

Of course, all this time I have to try and behave as if nothing's happening. A woman has come over to talk to me and I have to keep answering her in a normal voice. I must do nothing to give away the fact that I'm not actually standing beside her anymore but, instead, sitting crouched up with my bare sex split open into a great O.

Now, the dwarf moves round to stand in front of me. I feel his head push between my inner thighs. He presses his face into my lips and begins to lick me. He laps his tongue up and down and round and round until every part of my vulva and the whole of his face is sopping wet. When I look down now I see a little bulge in the front of my skirt where his head is. I have to keep smoothing the material down with the palms of my hands to hide it and that just pushes his face into my sex as though I'm encouraging him. He starts to suck my clitoris and it feels so good the only thing I want to do is close my eyes and moan out loud with pleasure.

I can't concentrate on what the woman is saying to me any more. I just keep nodding my head and smiling when she does; keeping up the act. I'm split in two halves – from the waist up I'm completely respectable and ladylike, but below that line, beneath the skirt, I'm doing something that's so shamefully obscene, it's depraved. I'm getting very excited now. My sex is so wet, I'm amazed the woman can't hear the sound of it being licked. I know I'm going to orgasm soon.

It's then I see The Stick glaring at me from the other side of the dance floor. I see from her face that, somehow, she knows straight away that I'm really aroused. She starts to hurry angrily across the ballroom to get at me, but there are so many couples dancing she can't push her way through. I watch her fighting her way through the crowd, getting nearer and nearer every moment. But I'm so close now I only need just a few more licks and I'll be there. It's going to be a race between us.

I pull the dwarf's face into me with both hands. I'm on the edge now and The Stick knows it. She realises she can't reach me in time so she just shouts out, 'Stop it, Amande!' Every single person in the room turns to stare at me.

The dwarf hears her too. And in a flash he pulls away from me and disappears back down through his trap door, closing it up neatly behind him. I'm left on my own, bound to the pole, unable to release myself.

In her madness to discover what I've been doing, The Stick runs over and grasps the hem of my skirt in her fists. She tears it away and the whole skirt rips off to reveal me lifted up into the air by this strange sexual apparatus, squatting splay-legged with the folds of my gaping sex blooming out between my legs like a red rose.

A great gasp goes round the room as I'm discovered. But it's too late now. Even though I'm not being touched any more I feel the orgasm starting inside me. I can't hold it back. I call out, 'I'm going to come! Don't look! I'm going to come!'

Of course, no one turns away. They all stand and watch as the orgasm begins to sweep over me.

I start to jerk backwards and forwards on the saddle and it makes every man there become instantly erect. And, although they try desperately to hide it, I know all the women are secretly sighing with jealousy at the way I climax so excitingly. They all pretend to be shocked and outraged to see me coming like that, to hear me crying out in ecstasy, but I know they'll all be thinking about it when their husbands mount them as soon as they get home.

And then, I'm waking up – lying on the bed, sheets feverishly thrown back. Totally wet with perspiration, wet with excitement. But *I am* coming! Really coming!

Under cover of dark night, I writhe around in silent rapture, slithering my body over the sheets. Out of reach inside its padded prison I feel my clammy sex clenching and pulsing wildly. My body finally takes control. It releases itself from all the pent-up sexual tension and frustration that's been building up inside me for so long and orgasms me ruthlessly.

Chapter 11

It says something about the awfulness of my existence that when The Stick informs me that I am going to accompany her on a visit to Nantes to hear a famous minister preaching, I actually look forward to it.

As Nantes is some fair distance away we are even going to get to stay there overnight. Not that she has any intention of letting me enjoy the trip, though. She's made absolutely sure of that.

We are to travel there on Saturday, spend the night quietly at a Christian hostel that has been recommended to her, hear the preacher on the Sunday morning and then return that same evening.

On the day of our departure, her old coachman drives us down to the highroad to wait for the stagecoach to pass. Disappointingly, when it arrives I board it to find The Stick and I are the only passengers. The old woman can hardly disguise her pleasure at seeing my hopes of having some interesting company for the journey dashed. As we set off she settles down smugly with some religious pamphlets whilst I'm left to gaze idly out at the scenery.

The morning drags by slowly. It is summer, but the day is overcast and showery, the passing countryside drab and grey. The road is rutted and uneven and it makes the coach jolt around endlessly so that even sitting is uncomfortable.

At midday we eat the plain, dry lunch that the cook has prepared for us.

I am about to resign myself to an afternoon of total boredom when, unexpectedly, we hear the driver reining in the horses and pulling up to a halt. It's obvious another passenger wishes to board the coach and I wait excitedly as we come to a standstill and the door of the carriage is flung open.

A tall, black-haired man climbs in and sits down opposite me. The Stick gives him a look that would wither plants, but there's nothing she can do, no matter how much she dislikes it she's powerless to stop him sitting there.

Even so, when he tries to make a few attempts at polite conversation, she soon manages to freeze him into silence. It's only a short time before he gives up and turns his attention to staring out of the window.

It gives me a good chance to look at him unobserved. He must be about thirty; skin tanned brown by the sun. He's wearing a heavy oilcloth coat, wet from waiting for the stagecoach in the light drizzle that's falling now. His eyes are dark blue, his hair long and gathered back with a thin bow in the fashion of sailors. In my mind I decide that's what he is – a seaman at home on leave.

As the afternoon wears away I lose myself in imagining the sights and adventures he must have seen on his travels.

It pleases me greatly that I can sense The Stick is almost beside herself with agitation. She hates the idea of me being so close to a man like this. She doesn't take her eyes off him, glaring across the carriage like a guard dog.

But we were up very early this morning and travelling in the coach is very tiring. Try as she might, I can see she is having trouble staying awake. Three times I see her head

The Pleasure Ring

nodding forward and then snapping back. And then, on the fourth time, it sinks forward and stays there. It's only a little while before the silence of the coach is broken by the rhythmic wheezing of her snores.

The sailor turns from the window and smiles at me. He nods across towards The Stick. 'Is she your friend?'

'Hardly that!' I snort indignantly. 'She is my chaperone. My husband insists she goes everywhere with me.'

He reacts to this with undisguised interest. 'It is, indeed, an intriguing woman that needs to be guarded so closely. You must have done something very terrible!'

I catch his eye for a second and a spark of attraction flashes between us.

And with that look the atmosphere in the carriage changes. I know he senses it as well for he begins to flirt with me quite openly, asking me all sorts of questions; where we've come from, where we're going, how long we're staying in Nantes; all the time trying to get me to reveal the dark secret of why I need to be watched over so strictly. I answer him politely but elusively, teasing him with half-truths whilst I find out things about him as well. I discover that his name is Jean-Michel, that I was right, he is a man of the sea, but not a common sailor – for he claims to be the captain of a tradeship.

At length, he leans forward and asks quietly, 'May I inquire, madam, are you going to meet your husband in Nantes?'

I shake my head. 'No, he is away at the moment, he has been away quite a while.'

Those deep blue eyes of his stare straight at me. 'It must be very . . . "difficult" . . . for you, not having his company. You have the look of a woman who is missing the attention of a man. Tell me, how long is it, exactly, since you were last parted?'

His double meaning is clear and fully intended. I feel my face redden at the boldness of his words and yet I'm unable to resist the temptation of answering him in the same way. 'I regret to say it's been a little over three months now. It has been a very unsatisfying time, but I have been helpless to do anything about it.'

The eyes widen in disbelief now. 'Surely in all those weeks an active young lady like yourself has found some way to relieve that frustration. Are there not certain pleasant activities that you could have privately indulged in?'

I have no doubt at all what he's hinting at but, in some strange way, I almost feel more embarrassed at having to confess that I haven't masturbated for three months than to admit that I have. It would be like an open admission that I'm on heat, needing sex badly.

'My chaperone is very attentive, sir. She sees it as her duty to ensure I never feel alone.' Pride makes me add, 'I assure you, though, it is for that reason alone that I have not turned my hand to more rewarding pursuits.'

I see him choosing his next words carefully.

'When your free time is so short perhaps it would suit you better to take some sort of vigorous physical exercise. I have been told one particular type of "riding" is very good for relieving the kind of tension you must be suffering from.'

He is very forward. Let us see how far he is willing to take this game!

'I think you are very right, sir. A good session in the saddle is exactly what I need.'

I pretend to look out of the window at the weather. Despite the rain that's falling I turn back to him and say to his face, 'In fact, sir, I do believe that right now

The Pleasure Ring

would be an excellent time to put your suggestion to the test!'

I see him shifting slightly in his seat. When I look down I'm pleased to discover he has a very obvious and plainly uncomfortable erection pushing out of the front of his britches.

He looks over to The Stick apprehensively. 'Such activity would be very hazardous.'

'I have always found, sir, that danger only increases the pleasure gained, don't you agree?'

I keep my eyes fixed on his groin. 'Of course, one would have to be absolutely sure first that the mount was worth the risk.'

I see him swallow hard. There's a long pause and then, very slowly, he reaches down and starts unbuttoning the flies of his straining pants.

Covering his crotch with one flap of his long coat he opens up the waistband and quickly frees his hard shaft into the open air. It seems to grow even larger as he cradles it in his palm, stretching and straightening to point out at me impressively. I feel my sex go wet. I can see I'm going to get a ride to remember.

We have no idea how long The Stick will stay asleep. There's no time for any foreplay, no time for anything else but fast, urgent sex.

He stands up and makes me turn round to kneel on my seat, facing away from him with my head pressed up tight against the cushioned headrest. I'm right beside The Stick, inches away from her slumped, slumbering body.

He hitches my skirt high up over my buttocks, rucking it up over the small of my back, exposing the two globes of my rear.

I thank God that I've somehow managed to persuade

The Stick to let me travel wearing loose-cut knickers rather than that horrible corset contraption I usually have to put on.

His fingers slide inside the waistband and I quiver as he tugs the soft peach silk of them down to my knees. Even before his hands leave them I feel his hardness pushing between the pouting lips of my sex and I quickly move my hand down inside my thighs and guide him into me.

I've almost forgotten how good it feels to have a man inside me, to be opened up by the stab of a cock.

My fingers stay between my legs. Shamelessly, I start to excite myself as he takes me. His own hands slide under my short travelling cape to find the ties on my bodice. He loosens the tight lacing enough to ease my breasts out so that he can cup them in his palms and tease my nipples with his thumbs.

I bite my lip to stop myself from making any noise, but it's no use. The carriage is swaying so violently that it keeps rocking us together in all sorts of unpredictable and unexpected ways, keeps making him go into me from new, different angles. And when he does that I just can't help letting out sharp little moans of pleasure that make The Stick stir in her dreams.

Knowing that any one of my cries could waken her, Jean-Michel feverishly works my knickers down past my knees and off me. He folds the light fabric in his hands and then forces it into my mouth as a sort of gag and bitepiece combined.

I grip it tight between my teeth. Now, only the shaking of my head gives away the force of the mounting he starts to give me.

I can tell he's going to come soon. I hold back my own pleasure, trying to time my climax to match his. He's

The Pleasure Ring

plunging into me now, standing with his legs spread apart, shafting his cock in from end to end. It won't be long. I feel the glow of orgasm starting to grow inside me. I'm on the edge, only just in control. A few more strokes and I won't be able to hold back.

Then, suddenly, the coach wheel goes over a boulder in the road and the whole carriage lurches violently. It makes Jean-Michel lose his balance, makes him ram his cock into me so hard it lifts me off my seat and tips me over towards The Stick.

And it's too much. I can't help myself.

It's such a deep powerful stroke it makes me come off. The orgasm just happens inside me and I come so wonderfully I can't restrain myself. My mouth falls open, the gag drops out and I groan loudly right into The Stick's ear.

To my horror I see her starting to rouse. We only have seconds to cover ourselves up before she'll see us.

Even though I'm still coming I have to spin round in my seat, madly smoothing my skirts down, pulling my cape closed over my bare breasts as best I can. With great presence of mind Jean-Michel snatches my knickers off The Stick's lap before he throws himself back into his seat. He just manages to wrap the flaps of his coat over his crotch as her eyes flicker open.

I sense her glowering around the carriage, incredibly cross with herself for having been so negligent, searching us with her eyes to try and discover if we've taken advantage of her lapse. I turn my face away from her, pretending not to notice she's awake, buying time to let the pulsing flush of orgasm pass over me.

Jean-Michel is sitting back in his same seat, diagonally opposite The Stick, right in the other corner of the carriage.

She settles down to watching him again, but the light is failing now as evening falls. Soon I can tell he has become nothing more to her than a shadowy figure half lost in the darkness. But I can still see him alright!

Of course, he never got to come when I did. I imagine how pumped up his cock must be now. It gives me a thrill to think of it just there under his coat flaps, still standing red and hard, absolutely bursting with spunk.

I feel a light tap on my ankle. With careful nonchalance I turn my head slightly to face more towards him. I let my eyes drift round to meet his and as soon as he catches my glance he motions for me to look downwards.

I watch, wide-eyed, as he slides his left hand into his outer pocket and very slowly raises the coat flap up. He makes it into a little screen between his crotch and The Stick, but holds it at an angle that still gives me a full view of what he's doing.

Sure now that his lap is hidden from The Stick's sight, he carefully lets the other coat flap drop away to reveal his thick penis. It's just as I'd imagined it, thrusting out of him like a crimson staff.

He lets me look at him for a while and then, as I stare in amazement, he scrunches my knickers up into his hand and, right under The Stick's nose, begins to silently massage the end of his cock with them, furtively rubbing the soft material over it just as if he was polishing up a big, smooth brass doorknob.

I can see from his face what the sensations are doing to him, the way he can barely stand it. But we're nearing the outskirts of Nantes now. It can't be long before we arrive at the coaching stables. I want to help him come, excite him some way to aid him reach climax. Turning my body father away from The Stick I secretly fold up the hem of my

The Pleasure Ring

cape to expose my still bare breast to him. I hitch it right up so that he can see my cherry-hard nipple set on its pillow of soft, pale flesh. My heart is pounding with fear. I'm so afraid that someone in the town will look into the coach and see us both displaying ourselves to each other in such a lewd way. We could be caught and arrested!

Time after time we pass under the glimmer of house lights and the darkness is pushed back enough to show his palm rolling, ever faster, over the top of his shaft. Then I look out to see the coach house up ahead. There are only seconds left. His hand becomes a blur now, desperate to relieve himself before we arrive.

And just as we turn into the stables, he makes it. Even though he has to hide it, I see him jolt forward in that way that men do when the first spurt comes. I look down at my knickers in his hand and see the gathered material suddenly billow out as his spunk jets into it.

Moments later, we draw to a halt. Even though he hurriedly draws his britches closed, I'm sure Jean-Michel must still be loosing come when the door of the carriage is opened by the stable boy.

The Stick pushes past me to get out first. Out of sight behind her, I take the opportunity to squeeze my breasts back into my bodice as I smile conspiratorially at him.

Composed and in control of myself again now, I calmly get up to follow the old woman.

I leave Jean-Michel behind me, glazed-eyed and sprawled weakly in his seat, his trousers gaping open, the last drops of spunk oozing from his cock even now.

As I pass by him I retrieve my knickers with a pert grin. Then, tucking the hot, sticky silk bundle into my dress pocket, I deliberately walk away without a backward glance.

Chapter 12

Needless to say, the sermon I have to sit through the next day is mind-numbingly boring, an hour and a half of hellfire and damnation. Even worse, The Stick makes us get up really early so that we can be first in the church and reserve the front pew right under the pulpit. Of course, she thinks the preacher is wonderful and keeps on referring to him as 'a saint walking amongst us'. She just doesn't seem to notice the way the old goat keeps looking down the front of my dress all the time he was haranguing us.

We catch the late coach that evening, as planned. It's a beautiful warm night. The moon is shining, full and bright behind a shifting veil of drifting clouds. We soon leave Nantes behind, rumbling along through open farmland. Then we start to climb, rising up out of the fields onto high moorland. The coach goes slower and slower as the horses struggle up the long hill.

We reach the summit but, just as we breast the top, we hear the cry that all travellers fear most. From the darkness a stern voice shouts, 'Stand and deliver!'

Fearfully, I peek out of the carriage to see a masked figure on horseback barring our way and pointing a brace of pistols at the coachman. He pulls the horses up at once, feeling little urge to have a hole blown in him as his reward for trying to protect our meagre pickings.

Keeping one gun on the driver, the highwayman swings out of the saddle and approaches the carriage door. There are five of us in the coach altogether; a married couple, a man who looks like a lawyer and The Stick and I. The Stick is shaking like a leaf, already opening her purse to hand over her money. The door flies open and the second pistol is turned on us all. The man holding the gun is tall, dark-skinned and wearing a long, oilskin coat. Despite the mask, I recognise him at once – it's Jean-Michel.

And what's more he's come to take me away! My heart soars when I hear him announce with exaggerated politeness to the others that they need not trouble themselves. 'Tonight,' he says, 'I have come in search of a very different kind of jewel box.'

He gestures for me to get out of the carriage. The Stick starts wailing and shrieking, begging him not to take me. It's plain she has no idea who he is, has no inkling that this is not a kidnapping but a rescue mission.

He pulls himself up onto his horse and lifts me up behind him. Before we depart he forces the coachman to unhitch his horses. As soon as they're free he fires a single shot into the air and they all bolt off into the night, leaving the carriage stranded. With a great roar of laughter he reins his own mount round and we fly off across the heath like an arrow from a bow. I hold onto him tightly, not knowing where we're going or how we're going to live, just happy to be with him, happy whatever happens because I'm free as well.

I'm still surprised though, when he pulls the horse up only half a mile or so from the road. We're in the shadow of a copse of twisted hawthorns. Even so, I know the coach is only just out of sight over the last hill and I can't understand why he's stopped so soon. Or at least, not at first.

The Pleasure Ring

Without a word, he springs down out of the saddle and, pulling me roughly by the wrist, he makes me half fall down after him into his arms. I wrap myself around him, drawing him to me lovingly, telling him of my joy of being with him.

Firmly, but coldly, he releases himself from my embrace.

'I'm afraid you misunderstand the situation you're in, my little sweet. I assure you my intentions are purely *dis*honourable. I've stolen you away for a very different reason than you think. I want you only so that I can take you with me on my next voyage and have you whenever I feel the urge for sex. Haven't you realised it yet? I don't want you as my lover, I only want you for your—'

His eyes shine in the moonlight as he leans forward to whisper this last, most vulgar of words into my ear. He laughs at the way it makes me blush and then he spins me round to face away from him.

'Firstly, though, we have business to finish from yesterday. This will show you how it is going to be between us!'

Saying that he pushes his hand up the back of my skirt and, with one jerk, rips my knickers off me, tearing the silk apart at the seams. He pulls out his pistol again.

'Get back onto the horse!'

I have no choice but to obey. As soon as I'm on the beast's back he comes in front of me and, pulling me forward, knots a length of cord round each of my wrists. He quickly ties the two ends together tight round the horse's neck so that I'm bound as though I'm hugging it.

Next my stockings are pulled down off my legs and each of my feet is lifted up and guided into the bags that hang off both sides of the saddle. I'm left tipped forward, folded-up and bent double in a crouching position. My bare arse is spread apart uncomfortably over the front edge of the hard leather saddle; my quim lifted just clear of the worn knob of the pommel by the tightness in my leg muscles.

Jean-Michel climbs up behind me and pulls my skirts out of his way, making me naked from the waist down. His horse is a stallion and I can't help noticing how its ears prick back as it catches the scent of my split sex on the breeze.

The moment we set off, the movement makes me start to bob up and down in a way that repeatedly grazes my sex onto the pommel. Then he urges the horse to a canter and the knob begins to ride so far up into the hidden lair of my clitoris that I have to call out to him, 'No more, please, I beg you! No more, I can't stand it!'

I hear him laugh aloud. 'No more, my darling? But this is nothing yet!'

I groan to feel him unbuttoning his breeches, realising all too well now how he's going to have me. He eases his pants loose and places himself right behind me, holding himself just in the place where the continual jogging of the horse forces my vulva to cap the bell-end of his rolled-back cock.

Once I'm opened up, Jean-Michel spurs the horse on faster. And now the action starts to make me ride the whole length of his rampant shaft. He's going into me so strongly I can hardly stay on the horse. I have to grip its flanks tightly between my knees, but that just tightens my sex around his shaft and increases his pleasure.

He drives the stallion to a gallop and stands in the stirrups to mount me all the harder. Time after time my bouncing arse rises and falls to the pounding rhythm of the horse's hooves. Obscenely joined to him like this, I'm impaled again and again as we surge on, mile after mile, across the black, barren moors.

The Pleasure Ring

My clitoris is on fire, being tortured against the harsh kiss of the pommel. I'm going to be so sore. I pray it won't be long before he comes!

Frenzied with lust now, he starts lashing the horse on with the ends of the reins, thrashing them from side to side, not caring how he catches my own flanks with the stinging leather strap as he does it; shouting out into the night as he rides us both wildly.

Then, at last, I hear him call out in orgasm. And, at the moment of release, he pulls himself out of me and twists sideways in the saddle. I look back to see great snakes of spunk pouring from the end of his cock and being whipped away on the wind. One after another, the sticky trails of come jet out of him and then stream behind us like ribbons – each one yards long, each one lost in the darkness before it floats to the ground.

Chapter 13

We ride all through the night, arriving at the coast just before dawn. Jean-Michel brings the horse down to a disused net store tucked away on the outskirts of a small harbour. There are men there waiting for us, crewmen under his command. Unceremoniously, they bundle me into a huge sack. Three of them pick me up and carry me, struggling, along the quayside. Smothering my cries for help, they smuggle me up the gangplank and aboard his waiting ship before anyone else is up and around to see.

I'm locked below decks in a windowless cabin and left. As soon as they've gone I try to force the door. But it's no use. No matter how hard I try to rattle and snatch at the handle, it won't come open. There's nothing I can do. Finally, in tears of frustration, I throw myself down onto the bed.

The last few hours have been so long and trying, it's only a short while before I cry myself to sleep.

When I wake up, for a few moments I have no idea where I am. I can't understand why the bed is tipping from side to side underneath me.

Then the memories come back to me and I realise it can only mean one thing – the ship has sailed.

In a blind panic I rush back to the door again. To my

surprise, I find it's unlocked now. I go out into the gangway. There's a stairway just beside the door. Climbing up it and then up the next flight, I come to a small doorhatch and burst through it.

I find myself standing in afternoon sunshine, right up at the bow of the ship. I look out ahead. There's nothing but flat, grey water. I turn to scan behind me and, to my despair, I see the same vastness of empty sea stretching away to the distant horizon. It's obvious we've left land, and any chance of escape, far behind. No wonder my door had been unlocked. It's the ship, not my cabin, that's my prison now.

For the first time I become aware that I'm being watched. I look back across the ship to find the whole crew has stopped work to stare at me. Jean-Michel is standing up on the raised rear deck with the other officers. With a sweeping wave of his arm he calls out to everyone, 'Gentlemen! Let me introduce you to my new bed companion, Amande. You may all look at her as much as you like, but don't ever think of touching her. You must never forget she is mine alone, my own special property!'

He turns his attention to me. 'Amande, my dear, I do believe that you are a little overdressed for your duties onboard the ship. You may dispense with your skirts and blouse!' The tone of his voice tells me that he means what he says, that he expects to be obeyed immediately, here and now.

I stare around at the other men, willing one of them to speak up and spare me this humiliation, but the expressions on their faces tell me no help will come, that they all want this to happen.

Jean-Michel chides me, 'Come, Amande, be quick! Don't keep everyone waiting.'

The Pleasure Ring

With the utmost reluctance, I turn away from them all and start to unlace my top. I slip it off my shoulders and over my breasts. There is an audible groan when I have to let it fall down to my waist so that I can begin unhooking my skirts.

When they're undone I stay there holding the loose waistbands in my hands, unable to make the final move of letting them go. The cool wind has made my nipples stand as hard and red as cherries.

I remember with shame that I have no underwear on under the skirt. What will the men all think of me when they find out I've been walking around with my sex exposed so brazenly?

Jean-Michel calls out to me again and I sense the edge of anger in his words now. I take a deep breath and, with a single movement, I open my hands and turn back to face them.

As the folds of material slide to the deck, I stand before them, displayed to their wolfish gaze as naked as I've ever felt in my life before.

Chapter 14

You can imagine how I feel when I learn that Jean-Michel's ship, *The Fleur-de-Lys*, is expected to be away from France for at least a year. We're bound for the newly discovered Spice Islands that lie to the south of Africa. Jean-Michel intends to barter goods with the islanders in exchange for aromatic powders and seeds that he will then take to the ports of Arabia where they're worth their weight in silver.

We have nine weeks' sailing ahead of us just to reach the islands. Day after day, we plough through the never-ending blue waves, pushed on by the steady tradewinds. Day after day, the sun climbs up into the cloudless sky and burns down on us from morning till night. And, all that time, I'm not allowed to wear a stitch of clothing. Ever.

For the first few days I'm totally embarrassed at having to go about uncovered like this, but it's surprising how soon I become accustomed to it. In some ways I even enjoy it. With the sun being so hot it's often more pleasant to be without clothing and let the breeze cool me. The sunshine is turning the whole of my body a golden brown colour that, although very unfashionable in France, I rather like.

Even though they've been warned not to touch me, I have to take care not to arouse any of the crew unwantedly. In this heat few of them wear more than a pair of ragged trousers and I soon learn from experience that even bending over carelessly when any of them are behind me gives them immediate, undisguisable erections. I have to remember to bob down to one side so as not to show them too much.

During the day I have to cook for Jean-Michel and serve him his food in his cabin but, of course, it is the night hours he really wants me for.

Like everything else on board, our 'sessions' soon develop into a routine set by the strict timetables of the ship. Every evening he calls me to his cabin at a certain time and forces me to lie on the huge double bunk that's built into the wall. He makes me put my wrists in chains fixed into the head of the bed (not only so that I can't protect myself from his advances, but also to ensure that I have no way of injuring him when he's asleep). Then he leaves me restrained like this whilst he makes his final rounds of the decks before returning to begin on me.

Every night he strips his clothes off in front of me before blowing out the candle. Then I feel him climbing into the bunk beside me, his stiff member fitting awkwardly between us as he lies beside me and starts exploring my defenceless body with his hands and his tongue and sometimes other, even worse things, that I can't bring myself to speak of.

I'm powerless to prevent him from doing anything he wants to me, but I have my own way of paying him back for using me so badly.

No matter what he does to me now, I never ever give him the satisfaction of seeing that he's arousing me in any way. I lie motionless on the bed and pride myself on not showing any emotion. I let him mount me and pleasure himself as often as he wishes, but I give nothing of myself to him.

How he hates that! It drives him crazy. He's fully aware he could use his power to order me to moan out any number

The Pleasure Ring

of false cries of desire, to roll about gripped in the most ecstatic of faked orgasms, but we both know that they would mean nothing. The one thing he can't force me to do is to come for him the way I did in the carriage on the road to Nantes.

The mad thing is, even though I hate him for what he's done to me, I still find it hard to control myself when I'm with him. Deep inside me I realise now it was this wild, dangerous side of him that attracted me in the first place. He's such an inventive lover that I start to find it harder and harder not to let him see the effect he's having on me. He seems to know exactly how and where to touch and stroke and kiss me to weaken my defences and I must confess that he often uses his tongue on me in a certain way that makes me ache to come.

Apart from that first urgent time on his horse, he's always been very, very gentle with me. He takes me slowly and sensuously, desperately trying to arouse my desire. He deliberately builds himself up, little by little, until he's right on the edge and I know I only have to make the slightest of movements to tip him into orgasm. He waits there willing me to do it but, of course, I never have yet and he's always forced to bring himself off.

I soon find the best way I can prepare myself against his seductions is to masturbate secretly whilst he's away on his round of the deck. Even though my hands are tied up I manage to do it by using my feet to ruche the bedsheet right up between my legs and gripping it between my thighs. I cross my ankles and I rub my legs together frantically until the rough linen works right up inside my sex and chafes my clitoris to raw excitement. My comings are really hot and dry like that and I always have to fantasise hard to take myself over the edge.

As a way of getting at Jean-Michel I deliberately think about someone else on the ship – a man they call Zikko. He's a young, blonde-haired midshipman with a very sexy body. Whenever I meet him he gives me a look that just makes me melt. He's the only one I don't take so much care with if I'm bending over and I think he's watching!

Zikko is known for being good with his hands and one of his special duties is to repair all the tools and navigation instruments on board.

In my fantasy I'm below deck, walking along the passageway outside his little workshop. As I pass the door I hear a familiar noise coming from inside. A fast, but regular, beating sound that I recognise straight away. I stop and press my ear to the door, my only thought the arousing prospect of surprising him in the middle of the solitary act I'm so sure he's indulging in. I put my hand silently to the latch and then, flicking it open, I burst into the room.

I discover Zikko sitting hunched in his chair but, at first, I truly believe I've made a mistake. Laid out on the bench in front of him is the case of Jean-Michel's telescope. It's clear Zikko has been taking it apart to clean it. He has the narrow end of it standing up out of his lap and the noise I heard was just him polishing a cloth over the brass barrels, sliding the close-fitting tubes in and out of each other.

Feeling a little ridiculous, I start to apologise as best I can, but something about the way he's twisting his body away from me, the way he seems so reluctant to look at me directly, makes me examine him again.

And now I see why he's acting so shamefacedly!

His trousers are undone at the waist. He's not gripping the end of the barrels between his thighs, he's holding it pushed over his cock!

He's been exciting himself by pistoning the closed end

The Pleasure Ring

of the eyepiece in and out and sucking his swollen prick up and down inside the metal tubes.

I've caught him red-handed, red-faced and – best of all – red-cocked!

I close the door firmly behind me. He's in no position to protest when I walk over to his chair and prise his hands off the barrels to replace them with my own. I lean over him provocatively and I say, 'This is no less then you deserve. Let's see how much good spunk you were going to waste!'

I begin to pump the eyepiece, going much harder and faster then he could ever have stood to do it to himself. I show him no mercy at all. His eyes roll back and his mouth falls open slackly as I suck his cock far up inside the tubes again and again. He tries to reach a hand out to stop me but, before he can touch the telescope, I literally wank him to the floor. Drained of all strength, he slides limply off his chair and slumps onto the carpet. All the while I keep the end of the tube pressed tightly against his groin. I keep jacking his cock until he's laid out flat on his back.

Then, when he's almost fainting away, I pull the telescope off him with a disgusting wet sound and he groans aloud as he looks down and sees what I've done to him. I've sucked his cock out longer and thinner than any prick should ever be. It's standing up out of his horizontal body like the tall mast of ship. I just have to have him now.

He's so long I have to lift up on tiptoes to straddle myself over the end of him. I lower myself onto him gingerly and balance on the end of his spear-like shaft. Cupping my breasts in my hands I start to slowly bob up and down on what must be the most wonderful seat in the world.

I sink lower, squatting back on him, swallowing more of him inside me. I'm grunting and panting with the exertion of holding myself crouched over him, but there's no stopping me. He starts moaning, 'Yes! Yes! Ohhh! Yes!' and I know he's going to come. I push down on him all the way now, riding him until I feel the rounds of my arse ground on his thighs and I'm taking every inch of his elongated cock.

He starts to thrust up against me, but at the last moment I snarl cruelly, 'I said I wanted to see your spunk!' and I deliberately tip forward onto all fours to make his cock spring backwards out of me. It slaps forward again, missing my vulva and sliding up into the groove of my buttocks instead. I look back over my shoulder and see the head of it protruding up above my cheeks. Zikko moans in disbelief to find his cockhead suddenly bucking into thin air, but I just watch heartlessly as his hot come starts to jet up out of him, firing out so hard it shoots straight up and splashes against the ceiling.

I know that's so awful. I can't think why I should find such an idea so exciting. The fact is, though, it never fails to bring me to climax. The thought of Zikko's cock erupting into the air like that just makes me come into the bedsheets every time.

My clever scheme of self-relief is a great success. In all the nights it takes to reach the Spice Islands, Jean-Michel never again gets near to making me come, not once.

Chapter 15

For the past two weeks *The Fleur-de-Lys* has been moored in the lagoon of Marquisa, the largest of the Spice Islands. This place is like Paradise on Earth, a sun-soaked garden of wild fruits and berries, rimmed by sandy, palm-fringed beaches and set in a deep azure ocean.

Only two other European ships have recorded landing here before, but the crew have heard many tales told of this place. For once, they turn out to be true. The quiet, smiling peoples of these islands have none of the sexual taboos that we punish ourselves with. They see lovemaking as a gift of the gods, to be shared freely whenever, and with whoever, they wish. The men of *The Fleur-de-Lys* have taken little time in availing themselves of the favours so willingly offered by the beautiful, dusky-skinned native girls.

The Marquisians have no use nor need for clothes. They go about as bare as Nature intended and it is almost amusing that they view my own nakedness without comment whilst finding the trousers and shirts of the men so strange. As I am, without doubt, the first white woman ever to set foot on these shores, I do believe they now think all European women are in the habit of parading themselves unconcealed! I just pity the next white women to arrive here.

Out of spite, Jean-Michel has only allowed me ashore

twice since we arrived. This morning though, I have insisted I need to have a proper wash and, as fresh water is in short supply on the ship, he has grudgingly given me permission to visit a remarkable place that the sailors have discovered – a natural bathing pool, hollowed out of the rocks by a high waterfall.

One of the crew is ordered to row me ashore and then keep watch over me to make sure I don't try to escape. This man, Johnson, takes me through the forest to the falls, some quarter of a mile away from the main village. When we get there he points the pool out to me above where we have emerged from the trees and I climb up alone whilst he stays down below, discreetly out of sight from where I'll be washing.

The pool truly is as wonderful as I'd been told; a cascade of crystal-clear water tumbling into a sloping basin of smooth, sandy-coloured rock.

Laying my towel and wash bag on a boulder, I step down into the warm water until it's up to my waist. I begin to soap myself but, after only a short time, I hear the sound of voices in the bushes down below me. Wading to the side of the pool, I peer cautiously over the edge.

I see Johnson disappearing off into the undergrowth with an island girl. She is young but certainly no reluctant virgin. It is she that is leading him, drawing him away to some quiet glade where she knows they will be able to mate together undisturbed.

She walks ahead of him and I see that, just like many of the older island women, she is going about with a certain kind of long, wrinkled seed pod inserted right up into her sex so that just the stalk shows out of her. As she steps along the path, she continually jiggles the end with her

The Pleasure Ring

fingers, vibrating the pod inside her vulva, readying herself for their coupling.

The women here quite openly masturbate themselves with these pods. If they have any distance to walk they will pass the time by strumming the stalk as they go. On my first visit, I plainly saw two or three girls bring themselves to full orgasm this way. They seemed to think nothing of supporting themselves against their companions whilst the weakness of climax washed over them.

I blush a little when I see her touching herself that way. I must confess I have found the tree that these seed pods come from and have picked one or two for myself when no one else was looking. They're hidden in my wash bag and I fully intend to experiment with one of them the first chance I get.

For the moment though, I'm actually quite glad that Johnson has gone. I'm happy to be by myself for a while in this amazing place. I return to the centre of the pool and start washing myself in the sunshine again.

Suddenly, shadows fall across the water and I look up to see half a dozen of the young native men standing on the rocks above me. My first thought is to call out to Johnson, but I soon see these lads mean me no harm. They are smiling and joking together, pointing at me, full of youthful excitement at the sight of my strangely different body.

When they see I'm not afraid of them, they climb down into the pool to take a closer look at me. They seem fascinated by my soap and the bubbling lather it makes on my skin. They all laugh when I show them how I use it, wiping it up and down my arms.

Flirtingly, I pass the bar to one of them and let him rub it over my back. Before long the others join in and soon they're all standing round me in a circle, soaping my breasts and belly as well, boldly running their foaming hands over my body, even caressing me, front and back, under the water. It feels so good I can't help making little gasping noises of pleasure. They know full well that they're making me very aroused. Two or three of them start to touch their cocks at the same time as they're feeling me, discovering the delicious new sensation of tossing themselves with sliding, soap-covered fingers.

Then, the slipperiness of the suds seems to give one of them an idea. He speaks to the others and I see their eyes light up. They beckon me over to a deeper, calmer part of the pool and show me something down in the water. A foot or so beneath the surface I see a narrow, tapered rock ledge jutting out into the pool. The end of the ledge has been chiselled away to a point like an upturned thorn. Except that, right at the tip where the point should be, it's been carefully sculpted into a small, ball-shaped knob instead.

It is only much later that I learn from one of the native girls that this whole valley is no accident of nature at all but a creation of the islanders themselves. It seems that, over many years, they have landscaped this place into what they call their love garden; an idyllic trysting place full of secret grottoes and secluded hideaways, of delights and surprises. An area where every flat rock and tree root has been carefully positioned and arranged so it can be used in some special act of lovemaking.

At this time, I have no way of realising that this is one of the sexual follies of the love garden or that by actually coming here to the waterfall, I have unknowingly sent out what, to them, is the traditional signal that I want sex. When I smile at them out of politeness they just take that as eager consent for what they have planned for me.

The Pleasure Ring

Unexpectedly, two of the men grasp me by the thighs and lift me out of the water. A third one takes the bar of soap and pushes it up between the cheeks of my bottom, smearing the jelly softness of it all round my tight little anus. As soon as he's finished, the other two lower me back down, positioning me right above the stone knob. I feel it touching against my greasily lubricated opening as probing fingers dip into the water and guide me onto it. With a firm push, I'm forced downwards and the knob is squeezed all the way inside me.

They let me go entirely and I find myself lying back, floating half under the water, anchored only by the stone ball pushed up into my back passage. The effect is incredible. I feel as though I'm completely weightless, as though I've shed my body. I'm able to relax my head back in the water and let my limbs drift effortlessly in the currents around me.

Watching me like this has made all the men erect now. There are six red-tipped, brown-shafted cock-spears jutting out at me. With deliberate sensuousness I let my legs float wide apart to display myself to their stares.

I see one of the men taking something off a cord round his neck. It's a brown and white speckled cowrie shell, the size of a small pear. One end of it has been cut away and the inside hollowed out. I watch with exhilaration as the man pushes the empty shell over the helmet of his cock like a cover, instantly turning it into the most exotic instrument of sexual stimulation.

He steps into the deeper pool between my legs. I look down and watch the hard, shiny, curving seashell shimmering in the sunlight as it cuts through the water towards my mound. I feel the little fluted end of it probing between my lips and then I watch as it disappears inside me.

It stretches me right open but, even though it's fearfully large, it's so smooth it slides in with ease.

The man begins to move slowly. The sensation of the shell going in and out of me is almost unbearable. I've never, ever been opened up like this before. The other men close in around us and start to masturbate themselves as they watch him taking me.

Strangely, even though we're making love in front of all of them, there is no guilt or embarrassment in our coupling. The man moves without hurry, pressing the shell into me again and again with a gentle, natural rhythm, happy to be pleasuring me so. I'm being driven wild by the motion of being rocked backwards and forwards on the stone ball, but I feel no shame in the way it makes me moan out aloud each time he sinks his massively sheathed cockhead into me.

Now, one of the men slides his spare hand down across my belly to massage my special place. I sprawl back and gaze up into the tropical trees above me, basking in the sun's rays, lost in ecstasy. I sense my climax building inside me. Both men feel it too and start to go faster for me, thrusting deeper, kneading me harder.

I hear myself calling out to them, urging them to finish me, begging them to bring me to climax. The words mean nothing to them, but they understand anyway. The anguished pleas of a woman near to crisis are the same in any language.

And then, at last, I'm there. I jerk forward in orgasm and when I look down into the water around me I see the

The Pleasure Ring

wanking men starting to come as well. One after another, I see jets of cloudy spunk snaking out from the tiny holes in the ends of their cocks and then drifting away in the current like cannon smoke.

Chapter 16

Maybe it's the expression on my face that raises Jean-Michel's suspicions when I return to the ship. But, whatever it is, I'm not allowed ashore again before we leave the island.

Another two weeks pass before the holds are finally stacked full with the pungent spices the islanders have been harvesting for us in return for our barter goods. The sailors work slowly, trying to delay our departure but, inevitably, the unhappy day dawns when they have to weigh anchor and set course for Ishtar, the capital of the kingdom of Pernia and our first port of call on the coast of Arabia.

Thankfully, Jean-Michel has not required my presence in his bed during the time we're at Marquisa. In the custom of these islands he was offered all three of the chief's daughters when we first arrived here and he's much too busy bedding them in all the different possible combinations to need to turn to me.

Though he seems to have gone out of his way to flaunt his pleasuring in front of me. Whenever he's had the women in his cabin he's made me bring food for them and then arranged it that when I arrive I disturb him taking them in some lewd position. Once I entered to find he'd made the three girls bend over onto his bunk side by side, their bare rumps all in a row. The girls lay there giggling and laughing together as he stood behind them, shafting the middle one vigorously whilst fingering the other two, one with each hand. On another occasion I discovered him bringing the youngest (and, no doubt, tightest) daughter to a shrieking orgasm on his chart table. At the time her two sisters were helpfully holding her legs folded back over her head, her knees by her ears and her sex presented over the edge of the table like a downy peach.

It's not until we're out at sea and he's had to do without them for a few nights that he starts to want me again. But, now, with my frustration satisfied by my adventure at the pool, I've been even more determined not to give him what he wants. The yawning gap between the sensual willingness of his young island trio and my own frigid, coldness has stretched him to breaking point. Yesterday evening, after a particularly unsuccessful attempt to arouse me, I think he finally snapped.

Tonight he has issued some very strange commands to the crew. He has ordered that there is to be no change of watch at midnight. When the early watch ends everyone is to go below decks until morning. He tells them all that the weather is settled and the winds light – the ship will sail itself well enough for those few hours. Even so, the men don't like it at all, don't like the idea of the ship running blind through uncharted waters just because the captain has got some crazy idea into his head. There's much murmuring and dissent, but Jean-Michel has a devil in him and he won't be swayed.

He keeps me with him in his cabin all evening, pouring him glass after glass of rum. I know there will be no opportunity to bring myself off before he has me tonight. If, indeed, having me is what he intends.

The Pleasure Ring

When midnight comes, he drags me onto the decks and forces the crew to their quarters. He has to draw his pistol before they finally do as he commands.

There's only the two of us left now. It's very eerie, so strangely deserted. Just the sound of the creaking of the rigging and the never-ceasing slapping of waves breaking against the prow of the ship.

Jean-Michel is acting like a madman. He puts his face to my ear and whispers drunkenly, 'I've finally worked out the reason I've not been exciting you. I've been doing it all wrong, haven't I? I've been too easy with you, too gentle. What you really want is a man who's rough with you, don't you? You just want to be filled with really hard cock. And that's what I'm going to give you! All day long I've been standing out here with an enormous hard-on, planning all the different places I'm going to take you. You're going to remember this evening for a very long time, Amande. Because, tonight, you're going to get what you really want. Tonight, I'm going to tie you up and shag you from one end of this ship to the other!'

He pulls me over to the ship's wheel. It's a giant thing, at least a foot taller than me. It's been lashed tight, fixed for the night to steer the ship on the same, steady heading. But other ropes have been tied to the worn-smooth wooden handles as well, four of them knotted at opposite points, top and bottom.

It's too dangerous to struggle. I submit without complaint as he binds my wrists and ankles to the ropes, spreading me out facing towards the wheel, the brass hub in the centre pressing into my belly and forcing me to bend out backwards towards him.

He stands back for a moment to look at me in the moonlight. Then I hear him pulling his clothes off. He starts to pace back and forth behind me, snorting like a raging bull as he masturbates himself to readiness.

And then, without warning, he covers me, pushing a cock into me that feels like a rod of iron. Reaching under my armpits he grips a spoke of the wheel in each hand and begins to hump himself against me, using his grip to thrust himself forward with all the force he can.

In the only way I have left to show my resistance, I turn my face away from his and I gaze down stonily through the spokes of the wheel onto the darkened deck below me.

Right at the far end there are barrels piled up in rows. They stand two high, against the wall of the forward bridge, holding all the extra spices that wouldn't fit into the hold. I try and concentrate my eyes on them, wanting to distract myself from what Jean-Michel's doing to me.

It's only because I'm staring so hard that I see the movement in the shadows. For a second I'm not sure, then I see it again. There's no mistake. Someone's down there watching us!

One of the crew must have found some way to climb out from down below and get into the narrow gap behind the barrels. They're standing right in the corner by the side of the ship, but there's so little space there they can't hide themselves completely. I can still see their head. I catch a glimpse of long blond hair and I know now it can only be one person – Zikko.

He's taking the most terrible chance. If Jean-Michel catches him there's no telling what he'll do to him. I don't even understand why he's running such a risk until I notice the thing that's sticking out sideways from the barrel beside him. At first I think it's only the end of a broom handle that's been left there. But it's not that at

The Pleasure Ring

all. My clitoris gives a great throb of excitement when I realise it's something else entirely – it's Zikko's cock.

He starts to rub himself hard as he spies on us through a gap higher up in the barrels and my nipples go hard at the sight of his shaft wagging up and down so vigorously. I feel my sex tingle with lust, unwantedly tightening on Jean-Michel's shaft.

And Jean-Michel senses it too. Deluded that it is his harsh handling that has finally brought me to excitement, he begins to plunge into me deeper still, reaching round to knead my clitoris under his fingertips.

I'm wet on his hand, but it's the thrill of deceiving him so that's making me like this.

He calls out, 'I have you. I have you at last!'

I shout back, 'No! No! Never!' But I know I'm lying now. I'm getting carried away watching Zikko silently wanking his beautiful cock. I'm losing control.

What happens next is all my fault.

I should have been more careful, not looked straight at Zikko for so long.

It's only a matter of time before Jean-Michel realises I'm staring at something. He only has to follow my eyes for me to give away Zikko in his hiding place. And when he discovers that this is what's really exciting me, he goes absolutely wild.

With a roar of anger he pulls out of me and jumps down onto the deck below in one great bound. He hurls himself at the barrels, scattering them out of his way in his rush to get at the man who has defied his orders and humiliated him so.

Zikko turns to defend himself and the two of them lock together, grappling, naked, round the deck.

There's nothing I can do to stop them, I'm still tied

firmly to the wheel. All I can do is watch – and what a sight it is.

For, as they wrestle together, I can't help seeing the way their two half-come cocks are still standing erect. All the effort they're putting into their fighting is keeping their pricks pumped up unnaturally hard. Their two blades keep accidentally striking against each other, fencing and parrying like duelling rapiers. And even though they're too desperately engrossed in their brawl to notice it, their 'cock-fight' is making them bigger and redder all the time, making them lose little beads of clear syrup from their tips. It's very exciting to see.

Neither of them is paying any attention to me. They don't notice me lift my hips up and wedge the hub of the ship's wheel against my crotch. I let the cold brass of it kiss my sex lips as I press myself onto it harder, furtively swabbing my oily clitoris backwards and forwards over its metallic smoothness.

I watch Zikko especially because his weapon is standing the stiffest, the most dangerously hard now. Yet he seems totally unaware of his overexcited erection until, suddenly, in the midst of all the heaving and grunting and groaning, the tightening sensation in his groin alerts him to the imminent event. He looks down, too late. To his horror, he sees his cock jerking up and down of its own accord, oozing out jelly-thick, white spunk. As they struggle together, long trails of it get wiped all over Jean-Michel's belly and soak into the black mat of hair at the root of his shaft.

I reach a shuddering little orgasm watching how it squeezes out of Zikko so thickly. It's more like some kind of pure secretion of male virility than sexual come.

And, of course, once Zikko's spunked like that his strength is sapped. Jean-Michel quickly manages to bring

The Pleasure Ring

him down and clamber on top of him. He holds him pinned down on the deck with his arm twisted right up behind him. In a shameful act of betrayal, a second, treacherous climax quivers through me at the sight of him kneeling nude over Zikko's back, his chest heaving and his sinewy body wet with sweat. I can't stop it happening when I look at Jean-Michel's crimson cock standing out of his bare thighs, knotted with veins and splattered with spilt come, looking more than ever like a victor's sword now.

For a moment I think he's going to do Zikko some real harm, but the passion seems to suddenly drain out of him and he calls out for the First Mate instead.

The Mate and two sturdy crewmen appear so quickly it's obvious they've been waiting right behind the hatchway, just bursting to come out on deck and find out what's going on.

They quickly bundle Zikko away and, on Jean-Michel's orders, I'm cut off from the wheel and taken down below with my hands tied behind my back.

Chapter 17

After a restless night, I'm collected the next morning by two crewmen and brought back up on deck. My eyes protest in the sudden brightness of the sun but I'm just able to make out the crew gathered together over to one side of the ship. I see Jean-Michel as well, standing apart from them, talking to the First Mate.

It's only as I get more accustomed to the light that I see that the Mate has a cat-o'-nine-tails in his hand. He turns to face me as I draw near, idly flicking the lead-tipped leather thongs backwards and forwards across the deck in front of him.

For one heart-stopping moment I truly believe Jean-Michel is going to have him whip me. But then I see Zikko tied up onto one of the huge rigging ladders that hold the mainmast steady. He's stretched out facing against the web of ropes, naked and bound hand and foot.

Jean-Michel breaks off his conversation and walks across to take my arm. In a voice heavy with sarcasm he says, 'Ah! Amande, there you are! Thank you for joining us.'

He leads me over to where Zikko is and starts to explain what he has planned for us both. It's simple, but obscene.

Jean-Michel is going to have Zikko flogged for disobeying orders but, in his warped, jealous mind he's thought up an extra twist. He's commanded that the whipping is to continue until Zikko orgasms. Or rather, until I make him orgasm.

The only way Zikko's punishment will end is when I bring him off in front of everyone.

Although that's awful enough, that's not the worst of Jean-Michel's depravity. He isn't going to allow my bonds to be untied. If I want to make Zikko come I'm going to have to do it with my hands tied behind my back – I'm going to have to do it with my mouth!

He doesn't wait for me to say anything, he just gives the signal for the punishment to start.

The Mate swings the cat up above his head, arcing it back behind him. Then his arm sweeps forward again and, like a swarm of bees, the tails hum through the air and spangle themselves across Zikko's clenched buttocks. He jerks hard against the harsh ropes, unable to hold in a low moan of pain.

What can I do? This is all my doing. It was me that encouraged Zikko by exhibiting myself at him. It's my fault he was discovered last night. I can't let him suffer for my wrongdoings.

There's a wooden hatch built up out of the deck in front of where he's strung up. I go over and kneel down on top of it.

Zikko's cock is right in front of me, pushing out through the square mesh of ropes. It's the only part of him that's on my side of the rigging. Somehow that seems to separate it from the rest of his body, makes it easier to do what I have to.

The Mate brings a second stinging stroke down across his arse and he bucks again. His prick jumps up at me as he does it, but this time it doesn't go down again.

It stays standing up out of the mesh, filling and growing,

The Pleasure Ring

rolling back at the tip. I look up at his face, but he turns his head away from me, unable to face the disgrace of being so visibly excited by the thought of what I'm about to do to him.

I bend forward, balancing awkwardly, bringing my face up close to his swelling cockhead. I don't know how to start, have no experience.

An inch forward and my lips touch round him, only the very tip inside my mouth. I begin to kiss him tentatively. But then, just when I'm expecting it least, the Mate lands another stroke on Zikko's behind and he jumps in shock. To the loud cheers of the crew his shaft shoots forward into my mouth and I become a cocksucker.

It feels so big, like taking in a whole, ripe plum on a stalk. I don't know what to do except suck on him at the same time as moving my head backwards and forwards. But that seems to be good for him. I feel him growing harder, bending upwards in erection.

The Mate starts laying into him faster. Zikko twists and turns in my mouth as the strokes land on him again and again. Sometimes he writhes so much he thrusts sideways, bulging out my cheek. I suck him hard now, urgent to save him as much pain as I can. I keep making a really crude slurping noise every time he escapes from my lips, but I can't help it.

His cock is shiny tight now. I've taken him to the edge already. His body goes rigid. He calls out, warning me.

I brace myself to pull back, to expel him before he climaxes. But as I try to move away, Jean-Michel lunges across and forces my head forward. He jams the whole length of Zikko's cock into my mouth, pushing it in so far I nearly choke on it. He holds me tight and I know he's going to keep me there until Zikko comes. I dread the thought of having to taste his semen, having to drink it down.

A final stroke of the lash is all it takes to bring him off. He can't hold back. His cock throbs violently and the spunk begins to pour out of him. It starts to slip down my throat, but there's so much I can't swallow it. I gag and gag.

It all comes back out my mouth and dribbles down my chin and I look a complete and utter slut.

Chapter 18

I'm kept locked up in my cabin for the next five days. No one comes near me except for one of the Mate's men who brings me my food. I ask him if he knows what's going to happen to me, but it's plain he's been ordered not to speak. Not that it matters really. In my own mind I'm sure Jean-Michel intends to be rid of me now, as soon as we reach Ishtar.

When I awake on the sixth day, I'm immediately aware that the movement of the ship has changed during the night. I can hear a bustle of activity on deck, sails being changed, rigging altered. By noon we are in quiet waters. My usual tray of food fails to arrive.

Sometime in the mid-afternoon the ship is shaken by a great, creaking shudder as we dock along a quayside. For a long time everything goes quiet but, as evening comes, I start to hear a growing babble of foreign voices, the shouting of orders, the heavy rumble of the cargo hatches being pulled back.

The ship is being unloaded already. How long will it be before it's my turn to be taken away too? I begin to pace around the floor, my stomach knotted in apprehension. Then I hear footsteps coming along the corridor outside. They stop at my cabin. I prepare myself for the worst, but I'm surprised to hear a voice warning, 'Stand away from the door!'

A second's pause and, with a mighty kick, the lock is burst apart. The door flies open to hang drunkenly on its twisted hinges and Zikko steps into the cabin.

He looks back nervously, checking both ways down the corridor.

There's no time for any greeting. He starts speaking straight away. 'Listen carefully. I can't stay long. Some of the crew found out Jean-Michel intends to sell us both at the slave market here in Ishtar. Luckily, I've got friends who weren't ready to see that happen. They were too afraid to cross the captain right out, but they've made sure I had enough help to arrange my own escape.'

He thrusts a small bundle into my hands.

'I got these things together for you. There's clothes in there and scissors for you to cut your hair short. Your only hope of getting away is to disguise yourself as one of the crew. There are a whole load of men up on deck helping with the unloading. What you've got to do is sneak out and join one of the lines waiting to be handed a sack from the hold. When you get given one, carry it down the gangplank on your shoulder so that it hides your face and then make a run for it, understand?

'I'll be recognised straight away with this blond hair so I'm going to slip overboard later and swim for it. But it's dark out there now. There's a good chance no one will notice you, especially when you're dressed up. Anyway, it's worth a try isn't it? What have you got to lose?'

I'm touched that Zikko should risk his own escape to rescue me as well. He's in a hurry to leave but, as he turns to go, I clasp his arm.

'Zikko, good luck! And thank you!'

He smiles for a moment and then he's gone.

I don't waste any time. I push the door to as best I can,

The Pleasure Ring

hoping that anyone passing won't notice the way it has been forced open. I have no mirror, only my reflection in the water jug to guide me with my cutting, but I manage well enough.

I pull on the baggy shirt and trousers that he's brought for me. It feels incredibly odd to be wearing clothes again after all these long weeks going bare. When I look down at myself, though, I soon see that further refinements to the disguise are going to be needed.

I take off the shirt again and, using the scissors, I slit a long strip off my bedsheet. I wrap it as tightly as I can round my chest, binding the giveaway roundness of my breasts flat down against my body. I rub dirt from the floor into my hands and feet and darken my face with it.

Now, when I put the shirt on a second time and look into the water, I can almost fool myself it's a young man that's staring back at me.

I've done all I can. Shaking a little, I go to the door and out into the corridor. I climb halfway up the stairway and peer out cautiously through the open doorhatch.

I look out and just beyond the side of the ship, so tauntingly close, is the city of Ishtar. Great arched warehouses huddle all around the harbour front, but through the gaps between them I glimpse the town itself. It's like nowhere I've ever seen before. White-painted, flat-roofed houses stretch away almost as far as the eye can see, some standing so close together that their fretwork wooden shutters touch their neighbour's across the busy thoroughfares below. Far in the distance lies the city wall and behind that a line of silvery sand dunes marks what must be the start of the vast deserts beyond.

There are people everywhere on deck, all working by the light of tar baskets hoisted up into the rigging. I stay watching as long as I dare, trying to make sense of all the confusion. I spy the lines of men Zikko told me about, slowly moving forward to collect sacks as they're passed up from below. I hold back until there are no crewmen from *The Fleur-de-Lys* amongst those waiting and then, taking my courage in both hands, I go out to join them.

I push in front of an old man with glazed eyes. He grumbles something in Arabic but I take no notice. I keep my face to the floor, willing the queue to move forward faster.

At last my turn comes and the sack I'm meant to carry is thrown to me. It's much heavier than I've imagined. I nearly stagger under the weight but have to hide my weakness. Gathering up every ounce of strength I can, I lift it up onto my shoulder and set off across the deck. I tread onto the gangplank. My legs are buckling under the strain but I tell myself every step I take is carrying me nearer to freedom.

Down onto the quay. Exhilaration. I'm going to make it! Going to make it!

Then, total despair.

The Mate is there, standing with an Arab merchant counting sacks as they come off the ship. No choice but to keep going. I walk straight past him. My heart's in my mouth.

Two, three, four paces past him.

A call from behind me. 'Hey! You there! Whose shift are you on?'

Ignore him. Keep going.

'You! Stop! Come back here!'

Footsteps coming after me. I spin round. The sudden shock of recognition halts him in his tracks.

'My God! It's you!'

The Pleasure Ring

I catch a glimpse of Jean-Michel on the deck above us, his attention drawn by the commotion.

In the split second it takes the Mate to recover himself I hurl my sack at him and knock him backwards off his feet. Then I run.

I hear Jean-Michel shouting, bellowing in anger. 'Stop her! Don't let her get away! A month's wages to the man that catches her!'

Half a dozen or more men peel away from the quayside in hot pursuit, the Mate at their head. I've got a good start on them though.

There's a gap in the warehouses right in front of me. And behind that a street thronged with people. I push into the crowds, trying to lose myself amongst them.

Everyone seems so alien; old men in long flowing robes, beggars in rags, women veiled from head to toe. I merge into the flowing river of bodies, letting myself be swept along until the current delivers me to the marketplace.

Now, I break free of the crush and set off, dodging and weaving along the aisles, hurrying past stalls laden with hunks of bloody meat, glistening fish, piles of strange fruits and vegetables. On impulse I dive down a side aisle. Every stall here is filled with leather goods; bags, saddles, belts and harnesses, all tooled with brightly coloured designs. Men sit cross-legged in front of their wares, laboriously stamping out the patterns. They look up impassively, following me only with their eyes as I rush past.

At the end of the stalls is a steeply sloping passageway. As I run up into it I look back. The men are behind me still! Closer now, gaining on me.

The smell here is awful. A tannery. Huge, foul-stinking vats bubble away on woodstoves lined down either side of the narrow, twisting pathway.

I hear the men arrive at the bottom of the passage. They're only yards behind me now. I come to a place where the track splits either side of a great iron pot, hung over a fire on an ancient wooden tripod. With a flash of inspiration, I kick the nearest leg, hard, as I go by.

It snaps in two and the frame collapses. The full pot crashes to the ground and topples over. A great torrent of boiling water spills out of it and courses down the passageway, flooding it from wall to wall. Moments later the air is filled with the screams and curses of the sailors as the scalding water flows over their feet.

It doesn't stop them, but it gives me time to get away, to get out of sight. The lanes are like a maze up here. I duck this way and that. But every turn seems to lead uphill.

I'm getting tired now, running out of energy. At last a passageway heading downhill! I dart into it gratefully.

It's a mistake. There's no way out. It's a dead end!

Too late to go back. I stare around me in panic. A doorway. My only hope. I shoulder it open and then push it closed behind me. I'm in some sort of courtyard garden.

Too exhausted to go any farther, I fall back against the door, eyes closed tight in prayer. I hear the men come into the entrance of the blind alley. Confusion. Voices raised in anger. And then, sweet mercy, footsteps turning back and hurrying on up the hill.

With an enormous sigh of relief, I open my eyes again.

Only to be met by the sight of two young Arab men, standing in an archway on the other side of the courtyard, staring at me excitedly.

Chapter 19

My first instinct is to turn and run, but the men don't seem to want me to leave. One of them smiles encouragingly and beckons me over. He speaks to me in Arabic, but I can't understand a word of what he's saying. He holds out a glass of wine and, though I hesitate for a while, I'm so thirsty I eventually decide to walk over and take it.

They gesture me inside. Cautiously, I pass through the thick stone archway into what must be their main room. It's obvious I've disturbed them eating their supper. By the yellowy light of the oil-lamps I can see where they've been sitting on a raised platform of rugs and soft cushions, their meal set out on a low table in front of them. The sight of food reminds me I haven't eaten since morning. The look on my face must tell them I'm hungry because they immediately press me to sit with them and share what they have.

Whilst I eat, my glass is filled again. And then again. I have no way of communicating except by signs and gestures, but I try to let them know how grateful I am for the kindness they're showing me. I keep attempting to explain to them why I'm dressed like this, why I was being chased by the sailors, but whenever I start to try they both wave me to silence. It's almost as if they don't want to know.

Whatever the reason, it's not very long before the wine

they're giving me starts to take effect. I begin to relax my guard, to let the dangers of my escape fade away. Without quite knowing why, I feel very safe here with these two handsome, athletic boys.

They drink with me and soon we all seem to be laughing at anything and everything. Then one of them goes off into another room and comes back with a very peculiar thing. It's a glass bottle capped with a covered metal bowl. The bottle's half full of water and there's a long, snaking hose coming out of it with a wooden rod attached to the other end.

I watch, fascinated, as the two boys light the contents of the metal cup with a taper and then sit back with me on the cushions. Looking at them whilst they're walking around, it's very evident they're not wearing anything else under their long cotton tunics. I can distinctly see their penises swinging to and fro all the time and I'm aroused to discover they're both a little hard.

There's a definite tension in the air now. They sit closer to me than before. One of them has the wooden rod. It's about a foot long, fashioned to resemble a string of smooth round beads. There's a tiny brass tube at the tip of it and he puts this to his lips and draws on it deeply, making the bottle bubble. He waits and then breathes out again, happily. It's only now I realise that this is some kind of smoking pipe, though the smoke coming from it smells much sweeter than the sailor's tobacco on board *The Fleur-de-Lys*.

The pipe is passed to me and, although I've never smoked before, I hold it to my mouth and suck on it just as I'd seen him do. The smoke is surprisingly cool and mild on my throat. I take it in and hold it for as long as I can. When I breathe out again my head feels curiously light.

The Pleasure Ring

As I lay back between them I can't help thinking how good-looking they both are, with their short dark hair, smooth olive skin and lean bodies. I'm sure they're both interested in me and from the looks that keep passing between them I just know they're planning something for later on. My only problem is going to be choosing between them. Or maybe that won't be necessary!

By the time the pipe is finished, I'm feeling really strange. Somehow, I seem to have taken a lot more turns with it than the other two. One of the boys tugs my sleeve. He tips his head sideways onto his hands and shuts his eyes, acting out 'Sleep'. He points to the room where the pipe was fetched from.

I feel a shiver of excitement run down my spine. He draws a shape in the air. A bed. A big bed. Maybe he's trying to tell me it's big enough for three, wanting to see my reaction. He laughs when I nod, shyly.

I feel so peculiar I need their help before I can stand properly. I know I'm not like this from drinking wine. Whatever was in that pipe has done this to me.

With the greatest politeness they light a candle and lead me to the room. They were certainly telling the truth about the bed – it is huge, with a massive carved headboard that goes halfway up to the ceiling. It's spread with rich covers and a collection of the most unusually shaped pillows I've ever seen.

They open up a second door and show me a tiny tiled washroom. One of them starts to close all the window shutters up tight and I just know he's doing it so that no one will be able to see or hear what we're going to do together. I'm feeling so sexy, I'm ready to begin straight away. I'm very confused when they turn and leave the room, smiling their goodbyes as they pull the door shut behind them.

Then I understand why they've shown me the bathroom. They want me to wash first! I've forgotten what a fright I must look.

I hurriedly strip the shirt and trousers off, unwinding myself from the uncomfortable linen binding I made on the ship. In the washroom I cleanse away all the dirt from my face and body and bathe myself ready for a night of lovemaking. When I come back into the bedroom, it's such a gloriously warm night that I pull back all the heavy covers and climb into bed under just one white sheet. I blow out the candle and wait in the darkness, naked.

I can hear them moving around outside the door and my breathing starts to get heavier. I've got butterflies in my stomach now, feeling horny with nervousness at all the things these two men might demand of me. My nipples are as hard as flint, tenting the sheet up into two rocky peaks. Expectation and fear mingle together, making my clit stand out the same way.

Whatever they intend to do, I want it to be good. So, for the first time in many weeks, I slip the pleasure ring from my finger and lock it in place round my swollen nub. It's wonderful to feel it on me again after all this time. Now, there are three little pinnacles of sensitivity pushing up into the sheet. All just aching to be conquered.

But as I lie there in the blackened room, the drug they've made me smoke begins to make my imagination run away with me.

I hear a sound and I convince myself it's the squeak of a secret cupboard being opened. In my mind I see the cupboard is full of leather whips and canes, straps and belts, all embellished with red and gold like the goods I'd passed as I ran through the market. I see them bringing out a perverted kind of harness seat from right at the back of the cupboard.

The Pleasure Ring

It's going to be so easy for them to overpower me and strap me into it. I'll be trapped in it and they'll attach it to this complicated system of ropes and pulleys so that they can winch me up and down over the bed. The seat has a hole cut in it that I can't help the lips of my sex bulging out through and they'll take it in turns to lie underneath me with their cocks pointing in the air whilst I'm lowered and raised onto them, hour after hour.

Or maybe it's some sort of wooden frame. An ancient Arabic raping frame that was designed for the public punishment of young girls who were caught whoring, but which has been outlawed in modern times because of what it did to the girls. They've had to keep the frame hidden for years, but tonight they're getting it out so that they can use it on me. They're going to put it on the bed and then lay me over it, lifted up in some way that allows them both to have me at the same time, front and back, without me being able to stop them.

Now I imagine that it wasn't a door at all. It was a game board being opened out. They're trying to decide which one of them is going to have me by playing some complicated gambling game. The winner is going to get to make love to me whilst the loser has to watch.

But more than that, before he comes in the room the loser has to insert a tiny, silver tube down the hole at the end of his cock. It's the length of a finger and the thickness of a grass stalk. He has to dip it in olive oil so that it's slippery enough to be worked all the way in until just the nozzle at the end is left sticking out. The tube gives him a constant erection but the weight of it makes his cock point downwards towards the ground even when he's really hard.

The loser will have to masturbate himself with the tube

inside his cock as he stands at the end of the bed. The winner will make me sit astride his cock, facing him, arranged so that I'm forced to watch. He'll ride me to orgasm easily, but my coming will arouse the loser so much that he'll orgasm as well.

And this will be the true forfeit of their game. For when he starts to ejaculate he'll have to pump all his spunk through that little pipe. It won't let him come normally, in slack, jerking spurts. Instead it'll shoot out of the pipe in a constant, needle-fine jet that'll be so powerful it'll go right across the room and write against the wall. He'll have to stand there for ages, groaning in agony as the tiny spray of come hisses out of him, on and on.

I'm making myself very wet thinking like this. I can feel the juice seeping down between my legs, making the sheet below me all damp. I won't forget to show them what they've done to me when they return.

The waiting is almost unbearable. I can feel my sex throbbing. If they don't come soon I might even climax accidentally before they get here.

The lamps are out in the main room now. I'm shaking with anticipation, but they make me wait . . . and wait . . . and wait.

I know they're there still. I can hear them. They must know what this is doing to me.

I listen hard, straining my ears as I hear a new sound. A constant slapping noise.

I can't stand the suspense any longer. Slipping silently out of bed, I tiptoe across the room and kneel down to press my eye to the keyhole of the door.

They're both in the centre of the room, on the thick, woven rug that's there. One of them is down on all fours and the other is standing behind him. The moon, shining in from a skylight above their heads, casts them in a glow of light in the otherwise darkened room. The standing boy's cock is very erect, jutting out of his wiry, naked body. Glistening with oil.

He enters the kneeling boy now. Slowly pushing in and out of him in a way that makes him have to grip handfuls of the rug in his fists to stop himself crying out.

How could I have been so stupid? How could I not have realised?

The craziest thing is that I might have been right about the secret cupboard if nothing else. The kneeling boy is not completely unclothed. He has his robe on still, pulled up and gathered over his back. But now he's been made to wear an elaborate tooled leather thong. It's fitted tight round his middle and up between his thighs. Two long, slender straps run back round the crease of his buttocks to end in buckles at the waistband.

The standing boy has the strap ends in his hands. He pulls on them again and again, shortening them, making them split the kneeling boy's cheeks farther and farther apart, stretching him more and more open. And every time the straps are tightened it pulls on his cock as well, distorting it upwards. When I first look his shaft is pointing towards the floor, but by the time the standing boy has finished with him, it's been swung right up to lie level with his stomach, just like a dog's prick. And the more the straps squeeze round the base of it, the further out of him it stands. By the end it's inches longer, taut and shiny, pushed out so far it's rubbing up against the edge of his raised robe.

I feel incredibly excited watching them. And incredibly frustrated. It's obvious they've nothing for me but I still feel so ready I'm going to have to do something about it.

The smoking pipe we used earlier has been put back in my room just by the door. I tug the wooden handle from the pipe and turn it upside down. Grasping it in one hand, I reach back behind my buttocks and push it into me like a giant dildo. I start to frig myself with it, feverishly ribbing it in and out of my slippery sex as I watch them through my spyhole.

The standing one's going to come soon. He keeps saying something to the other boy that makes him moan every time he speaks the words. I start squeezing my mound with my other hand, squashing the pleasure ring backwards. I make the tip of my clitoris catch against the undulations of the wooden rod as I abuse myself mercilessly with it, working it in my hand behind my raised rump like a horse jockey whipping his mount to the finishing line.

The standing boy pushes himself to the edge, until he can take no more. Then, at the very last stroke, he pulls right out and his bursting cock is silhouetted for me in the silvery moonlight. He arches back and milks himself over the smooth, dark skin of his lover and it looks just as though he's easing an endless string of liquid pearls out of the end of his shaft.

The kneeling boy gasps as they fall on him and then calls out. Without being touched once, his cock starts to jolt up and down as his own spunk flows. It spews out of him like water. But it flows straight into the thick cotton of his robe and just gets soaked up straight away. All I can see is a great wet stain spreading out in the cloth beneath his belly.

The sight of his spilt come being mopped up like that just makes me explode in orgasm. I feel my sex clench onto the pipe handle, gripping it hard. My whole body starts to melt round it. I feel stunned by the intensity of the climax, can't bear to take it kneeling like this.

The Pleasure Ring

I struggle to my feet and stagger over to the bed, the rod still clasped rigidly inside me.

Lights start to flash in front of my eyes. My legs turn to water. I can't control my body anymore. Then the mattress suddenly rushes up to meet my face as I fall forward onto the bed, unconscious.

Chapter 20

Someone is touching between my legs.

They're turning the pleasure ring, exploring it with their fingers. Maybe trying to steal it from me as I've been lying senseless. I knock the hand away, cursing angrily.

I'm completely amazed when a female voice responds in almost perfect French, 'That is hardly the proper way to address your new mistress, is it?'

My eyes struggle open. The bedroom is full of light now, the shutters pulled back to let the late morning sunshine stream in.

The young woman leaning over me is European, though she's dressed in Arab robes. Her accent is very good, well educated, but not native. At a guess I would say she's probably English.

Confused, I stammer, 'Who are you? What do you mean "new mistress"?'

She smiles, as though at some private joke. 'As to who I am, that is a long story. For the moment, it is enough for you to know that I am named Ladisa. In answer to your second question, I call myself your mistress for the simple reason that I have just purchased you from the man who's sitting on the couch in the other room.'

She gestures towards the door and I look through to see a repulsive whale of a man sitting there, the fat hanging off him in great folds. Even resting he has to continually mop his brow to wipe away the beads of sweat that keep trickling down his face.

'His name is Kalim and I've just paid him five hundred dinars for you. That's a lot of money. I hope you're going to be worth it!' She drops her voice. 'You do realise, don't you, that your two new "friends" deliberately drugged you last night? They did it to please Kalim. He is their keeper. He pays for this house and all the things in it, just as other men pay to keep their mistresses. You understand what I'm saying?

'When you arrived last night the two boys guessed quite correctly that you were a runaway from some visiting ship. But in the lamplight, with your hair cut so short and those sailor's clothes on, they mistook you for a young cabin boy. They offered you shelter and then plied you with hashish because, right from the start, they intended to give you to Kalim as a present.

'And what a rare gift you would have made! An untouched innocent for him to spirit away to his secret hideaway out in the desert. You must surely realise, now, what he would have done to you there? How he would have had you restrained so that he could force himself upon you without resistance. How he would have taken his greatest pleasure – hearing your cries of pain and knowing from them that it is he, Kalim, who has breached the tightness of your forbidden passage for the first time.

'You can imagine his anger when he was summoned here in the middle of the night only to discover you were really a woman. Perhaps you don't remember how clearly you were demonstrating that to them when they found you? It was certainly an unusual use for a hashish pipe!'

The Pleasure Ring

With a flush of embarrassment my hand dives down between my legs, but there's nothing there now.

She smiles again. 'For the sake of decency I took the liberty of easing the thing out of you just before you awoke. Only to find that you'd also been exciting yourself in another, much more interesting way at the same time.' Her eyes glance meaningfully towards the pleasure ring.

'Kalim was very disappointed but, above all else, he is a businessman. He knows that I am always in the market for beautiful young foreign girls. He sent for me, I liked what I saw and we struck a bargain over you.

'I should tell you, both he and I know all about your escape from the ship in the harbour. The crew are still turning the whole of Ishtar upside down looking for you. The choice you have now is simple. Either you can come into my service and submit yourself willingly to my demands, or else you can refuse and I will tell Kalim our deal is off. I have little doubt he will try and sell you back to the captain who's so desperate to find you. But I must warn you that Kalim is becoming sorely tempted by your boyish looks. It would surprise me greatly if he doesn't have some plan to take you to his hideaway before he returns you to the ship. Think what an arousing sight you would present to him. The unique delights of the smooth round buttocks of a reluctant boy-woman!'

We both know full well she's not offering me any real choice at all. I tell her I'm ready to go with her straight away.

Within five minutes she has me dressed in a full white robe similar to the one she is wearing. She swathes my head in a long scarf of bleached muslin and then fixes a veil across my face so that, in the traditional way, only my eyes show above it.

She goes through to speak to Kalim and I wait anxiously, dreading that he's changed his mind about letting me go. I can only guess at the 'demands' this mysterious woman intends to make on me, but anything will be better than to fall into Kalim's hands.

I breathe a great sigh of relief when I see her handing him a purse of money. Pulling her own veil into place, she calls me through to leave. I hurry past Kalim without meeting his gaze, only truly relaxing when we're out of the courtyard and retracing our steps back down the hill to the marketplace.

For the second time I enter the bazaar in disguise. Though, thankfully, on this occasion no one seems to pay me any attention. We pass on our way unnoticed, just two women amongst a thousand dressed exactly alike.

Then all at once, I catch sight of a face that fills me with fear. The Mate is coming down the aisle towards us, pushing people out of the way angrily as he blusters along, searching faces, hunting for me.

Our paths cross before I have time to avoid him. For a second his eyes bore into me and my heart stops beating. I freeze to the spot, expecting him to lunge for me at any moment.

But he's so drunk he doesn't recognise me, so dazed with rum he just looks straight through me and then staggers on his way, swearing to himself. Stunned by the luck of my escape, I watch him limp off into the crowd, one swollen, scalded foot wrapped in a great bundle of bandages.

We hurry on faster now. Out of the market and across the city, turning into one bustling street after another until, finally, I look up to see the road ahead blocked by a massive gateway. Two soldiers stand with swords drawn guarding the entrance.

The Pleasure Ring

None of the crowd venture anywhere near, but Ladisa strides straight up to them. They make to block her way until she drops her veil and shows them her face. The instant they recognise her they snap to attention and let us pass. My new mistress is obviously a person of some importance.

Walking through the gates is like entering a different world. All the noise and jostling of the town is left behind us as we emerge into the quiet of a marbled courtyard, just one secluded corner of the magnificent palace that now towers in front of us.

It's beautiful. High above the white, shining walls, gilded domes and blue-tiled towers gleam in the sunshine. Could it be that Ladisa owns all this?

I begin to feel a little afraid. I keep remembering her comment about always looking out for foreign girls. I hardly dare let myself think what she might want me for. If she has this much wealth and power, she could have anything she likes done to me here.

She leads me across the first courtyard and then across another and another. The sheer size of the palace is awe-inspiring. We turn under an archway and down a long open corridor. At the end she opens a door and shows me into a small room. It's simply furnished; a raised bed, two wooden chests, cushions set out round a low table just like the two boys' house.

She closes the door behind us.

'Take off all your clothes!' It's an order, nothing more or less.

Afraid of the unknown consequences of refusing, I do as I'm told. I undress carefully, draping each item of clothing neatly over the end of the bed as I remove it, not wanting to make her angry by treating them roughly.

When I'm finished, bare naked, she makes me stand in the centre of the room, hands by my sides. At first, she doesn't move at all, she just stays by the door looking me up and down. Then she slowly walks round behind me, out of sight.

I feel her moving closer. A hand slides under my bottom, cupping my cheeks, feeling the firmness of them. I flinch away from her touch but she says sharply, 'Stay still. I need to examine you.'

Her other hand slides under my arm and comes up to cover my breast, squeezing it slightly, weighing it. The first hand snakes round to take hold of my other breast and then, together, they glide down my belly and over my thighs.

She lets her hands roam all over me. I feel very confused. There's something very ambiguous about the way she's exploring me. I can tell she's trying to be detached and professional and yet her hands are shaking slightly, moving stiffly as though she's having to control herself all the time. Even her voice sounds strained when she finally declares, 'You're perfect, absolutely perfect!'

She releases me, allowing me to sit on the edge of the bed and pull my robe round me. She remains standing, preparing herself to speak. She begins awkwardly, eyes averted to the floor.

'It is time that I explained to you why you've been brought here. But, firstly, I have a confession to make.

'When I told you that I had become your mistress that was not strictly the truth. I only said it because it gave me a thrill to make you believe I was. The truth is I am in charge of you, but I am owned, just as you are now, too.

'This is the palace of Prince Hassan, ruler of all Pernia. The Prince is my master and it was on his command that I purchased you. I am his Procurer of Concubines.

The Pleasure Ring

'You see, Prince Hassan is not yet married. He is still a young man and, like all young men, he has strong sexual desires. I'm sure he would bed every girl in Ishtar if he had the chance, but under ancient Pernian law the Prince of the realm is allowed to choose only one woman each year to become his bed-mate – his concubine.

'For twelve months this fortunate female lives a life of luxury, showered with gifts. And all she has to do in return is allow the Prince to mount her whenever and however he wishes.

'In past ages there was intense rivalry to be selected for this enviable task. The princes of old had many beautiful girls to choose from, but it was plain that the most suitable candidate needed to possess another, more sensual talent in addition to good looks.

'So a simple test was devised. A competition to find the most highly sexed girl, the young woman with the greatest libido – the one who could be brought to climax the greatest number of times in one continuous session!

'By means of this Trial by Orgasm the princes were assured of discovering the girls who would make the most voluptuous lovers for the coming year.

'The problem with the present prince is that he has very particular tastes in the women that arouse him. You must remember it is only very recently that European women, like us, have been seen in Arabia. To the men here our tallness and our pale skin make us exotic objects of desire.

'Prince Hassan has become more obsessed than any of them. He insists he will only consider European women as future concubines.

'That was the reason I was originally brought to Ishtar – as a competitor. It may be hard to believe but, until four years ago, I was actually the wife of Lord Willoughby, the chief British envoy at the court of the Rajah of Afmiristan in Northern India. Through my own misdeeds I found myself alone on that country's borders and I was captured by bandits who sold me to slave traders. Thinking that I was going to be of great value they transported me all the way here to Ishtar and offered me to the Procuress of the time.

'I kept trying to explain to them who I was, that I was a free Englishwoman, but they didn't understand. It was then that I got given the name everyone here calls me by. I kept telling them my name was Lady Sarah Willoughby, but "Ladisa" was the only part they could pronounce.

'It was only later, when I had been paid for, that my little "secret" was discovered and they realised I was not going to be at all suited for the duties of the Concubine. I was lucky not to be sent to the slave market to be sold again. It was only my skill at languages that saved me. I became, first, the Procuress's interpreter, then her assistant and, finally, when she became ill, her replacement.

'Since that time it has been my duty to supply the required number of foreign women willing to undergo the Ordeal each year. This year's Trial is to take place in less than two months' time. I already have three other girls and the present Concubine waiting to compete, but I've been looking for one more.

'Now, though, my search is over. I've found the woman I've been searching for! You, Amande! You are going to become the fifth competitor!'

She sees my outraged expression. Only half-teasingly, she laughs. 'Don't look like that! You mustn't forget all those promises you made about obeying me if I bought you from Kalim. Remember, I own you now. You have to do whatever I say!'

The Pleasure Ring

She crosses the room to pull back a curtain and reveal a second room. It is a bathing chamber, tiled from floor to ceiling around a sunken pool of shimmering, blue water. Soaps, perfumed oils and towels are laid out around the edge, all waiting invitingly to be used.

'And my first command is that you must take a bath. Refresh yourself now whilst I go to inform the Prince of your arrival. I will have food and fresh clothing sent and you can rest until I return for you later this evening. Whenever a new competitor arrives it is the custom that a special entertainment takes place in their honour.'

She goes to the door but stops just before she leaves.

'We will talk more after this evening but I do have one piece of advice for you now.

'It's about the present Concubine. It happens that she is also a Frenchwoman, like yourself. Though she calls herself by the Arabic name, El-Marrach. It means "The Heavenly One" and I leave it to your imagination as to what part of her body she is referring to.

'But I warn you not to seek this El-Marrach out. She is a viper. She is determined to win the Ordeal for a second time and I believe she will stop at nothing to gain her goal. You should avoid her at all costs.'

A smile comes to her face again.

'There's one more thing I should warn you about. Tonight's entertainment is going to be very explicit – a display of female erotica. I hope you'll find it arousing because the evening also involves a little test you must pass. It's one that a surprising number of girls fail, though, from the evidence I saw this morning, I'm sure it will be a mere formality to you.

'You see, whilst you're watching the entertainment, I'm afraid you're going to have to show me you can orgasm!'

Chapter 21

Once I'm alone my first thought is of escape. But the reality of my situation is all too clear. Even if I could escape from the Palace, how long would it be before I ran into one of Jean-Michel's crewmen or, even worse, someone who would return me to Kalim?

I have no option but to accept the grim truth that, for the moment, I am safer here in the Palace than anywhere else. Even if that does mean having to pretend to agree to Ladisa's outlandish demands.

Things seem a little better after I've pampered myself in the cooling water of the bathing pool. I dry myself and lie on the bed to plan my next move but, still drowsy from the hashish, it's not long before I fall fast asleep.

It is early evening when I awake again. Whilst I've been sleeping a silk wrap has been laid out on the bed in place of my white robes and an enticing array of food has been spread out on the table waiting for me. Hungrily, I tie the loose gown round me and go over to the cushions to eat.

I'm just finishing when Ladisa comes to the door. She quickly sets about preparing me for the evening ahead, carefully making-up my eyes and pinning my hair back with combs. She seems very concerned that I should present myself as well as possible.

Finally, she's satisfied with me and I have to follow her

out into the darkness. I'm still not wearing anything but the wrap and a little pair of embroidered slippers. I have to keep drawing the silk robe back over my sex as the night breeze tugs at it, constantly trying to expose me. Torches light our way as she guides me through the many passageways and courtyards we have to cross to reach the inner palace.

Eventually we come to huge, iron-studded wooden door. Ladisa knocks three times and a face appears at a tiny grille, followed, seconds later, by the sound of heavy bolts being drawn back.

The door is pulled open and we're welcomed by a line of young servant women in traditional Pernian costume. Bows of greetings are exchanged and then two of the girls come forward to usher me away to a side room. As I go with them, Ladisa calls over, 'Don't worry, just do whatever they ask.'

Once inside, the girls start gesturing to me that I must take my robe off. Remembering what Ladisa has just said, I reluctantly let them slip it off my shoulders. In its place they dress me in a short-cropped chiffon top and loose pants of the same translucent cloth. The floaty silk is gathered in at my ankles, but the pants are only just held up by a single cord tied low round my hips. The material's so light and sheer my body beneath is hardly veiled at all.

As soon as I'm dressed they bring me out of the room again. Ladisa is there waiting for me. She is dressed exactly as I am and I can clearly see the roundness of her breasts, the dark triangle of her sex. I flush at the way she stares at me in return. I can't help noticing how very hard and pointed her nipples are.

A second door is opened and we're both motioned into a huge, circular room, lit by hundreds of flickering candles. The walls are black, the ceiling a marvellous dome of dark

The Pleasure Ring

blue glass. There is no furniture except for two richly draped divans, arranged together on one side of the room. They're raised much higher off the ground than usual and, even more curiously, they're not level but tilted up at a slight angle at the pillow end. The girls lead us both to the couches but, not quite sure what to do, I hang back until I see Ladisa climbing up onto the side of the divan and then lying back.

As I do the same she turns towards me. 'You must remember at all times that this entertainment is being performed in your honour. When the servants come to attend us, you must not interfere with what they do in any way. If it was thought that you were displeased, it would be reported to the Prince and they would be severely punished. You must relax and try to enjoy the display as best you can. Look up now, it's about to begin!'

I turn my gaze to the glass dome, high above. For the first time I notice that there is a thin rope pulled tight across the centre of the room from wall to wall. At each end, a small, curtained tent has been suspended just above the rope.

As I look, one of the tents is pulled open and a girl steps out of it onto the rope. She's dressed in a dramatic gold costume that glows brightly in the candlelight. Almost as easily as if she was tripping across a meadow, she skips along the rope into the centre of the room. Her balance and grace are breathtaking.

Just as she reaches the middle of the rope, the tent at the other end is flung back and a man springs out to block her way. The girl feigns alarm and turns back. Now, though, a second man emerges from the first tent, trapping her on the rope between the two of them.

They both begin to stalk towards her and, as they step slowly along the tightrope, they skilfully cast off their clothes. By the time they meet at the centre, her two attackers are naked, their penises fully erect.

Far above us, the rope sways to and fro as they take hold of the mock-protesting girl and begin to pull her costume off. It comes apart with theatrical ease, falling away in detachable sections to leave her entirely unclothed.

Underneath, her body is painted. Her feet, breasts and navel are blue and silver; her pubis circled with rings of red and gold in a way that grossly exaggerates the size of her sex.

The men move closer into her. With amazing skill they take hold of her and twist her down forwards. They pretend to force themselves on her. The man in front of her grasps her shoulders and pulls her head onto his shaft, the man behind kneels, pressing his face to her pushed back vulva and lapping his tongue into her.

It is now that the servants come to the side of the divans. A woman approaches Ladisa, but, to my dismay, I find it is a handsome young man that is standing over me.

Mortified, I have to steel myself and permit him to unfasten the tie on my silk pants and pull them down to my knees. I force myself to lie still as he takes a spouted brass jug and starts to trickle warm oil over my presented mound. He waits until the oil is dribbling down between my legs before he lays the jug to one side.

And then, beyond endurance, he turns back and begins to worm two fingers onto my clitoris.

I can stand no more. My hand darts forward to push his away. But Ladisa sees what I'm about to do and calls out to stop me. Reminded of her warning, I have no option but to let my arm fall back and give myself up to this man's probing touch.

He begins to massage me gently, expertly stroking my

The Pleasure Ring

slippery coated bud backwards and forwards under his fingertips. In spite of my overwhelming feelings of shame and embarrassment, I can feel myself stiffening and swelling as he fondles me. It makes it much worse that he's so good-looking. He's watching my face all the time, smiling to himself at my arousal.

The acrobatic girl on the tightrope is being taken by both men now. The second man is holding her by the buttocks as he enters her from behind. After a while the two men take hold of the girl's arms and legs and they lift her off the rope altogether. They support her curled up in mid-air between them and they start to rotate her slowly, swivelling her round and round. And all the while she's being turned over, she keeps one of them sucked in her mouth and the other in her painted sex, letting herself be spiked from both ends just like she were roasting on a spit.

For the first time I dare to look over to Ladisa. She is lying uncovered just as I am, being stimulated in the same way. The only difference is that her head is resting turned towards me, studying me through heavy eyelids.

It's obvious to me straight away that she is being aroused, not by looking at the entertainment, but by watching me being masturbated. Knowing that, I can't meet her gaze. I let my eyes fall away across her body.

And it is then that I see it. A sight that sends such a surge of excitement through me the manservant feels it through his fingertips and makes his eyes widen in surprise.

High up on the marble smoothness of Ladisa's pale, bare thigh the perfection of her body has been despoiled in the most barbaric way. At the very apex of the roundness where leg and hip meet there is a vicious weal of raised, tortured flesh. On that perfect point an exquisite curving design has been seared deep into her skin.

Lady Jane Willoughby has been branded!

She sees the look on my face and asks softly, 'You find my markings exciting, don't you?'

I can't deny it. I would never have believed anything so cruel could be so sexually stimulating. My tongue is loosened by the kneading between my legs. Before I can hold back the words in my head, they tumble out. 'Ladisa. They're beautiful!'

Her eyes flash with dark pleasure. 'The kiss of the brand was my punishment for breaking the laws of Afmiristan. I wonder if you can guess yet what my crime was?'

In my heart I know the answer. 'You were discovered making love to another woman, weren't you?'

She almost whispers the answer. 'Yes.'

She lets the fingers of her hand gently trace over the curving design, flinching sensuously at the unbearable tenderness of the scars.

'These marks are *santra*, a punishment and a sign. They are there as a warning to any man that may ever be preparing to mount me that I am a lover only of my own sex. It was by these marks that the Procuress learnt the secret reason I was never going to make a concubine.'

'But, Ladisa, if this happened in Afmiristan, why didn't your husband prevent it? Why didn't he speak to the Rajah to stop this being done to you?'

A bitter smile comes to her lips. 'My innocent, it was my own husband that brought the charges against me!

'I have known where my true desires lay from an early age, but I was forced into becoming Lord Willoughby's wife by my parents. I had many female lovers before I married him and I didn't stop afterwards. I was unfaithful to him right from the start, even on our honeymoon. One night he came to my dressing room to take me down

The Pleasure Ring

to dinner and I couldn't let him in because I was still undressed and halfway to climax. I had to call out some excuse through the door as I stood there, leant back with my bare bottom pressed against the cold glass of my mirror, being taken to pleasure by the tongue of a very excited young chambermaid.

'In all the time we were married, we hardly ever shared a bed together, but he was such a passionless, unfeeling man I don't think he ever questioned the reason why. He was so insensitive he never suspected a thing about my illicit liaisons. I was always very careful – that is until the fateful afternoon in Afmiristan when he returned home unexpectedly from a visit to a nearby town.

'None of the servants were there to meet him because I'd sent them all away for the day. He wandered around the empty house until he was drawn upstairs by the sound of distressed moaning he could hear coming from my bedroom. He rushed in expecting to find me suffering from some kind of fever but, instead, he discovered me on the bed with one of the ladies of the Court.

'You know, the Afmiris have a special word for a woman's sex. They call it a *yoni*, but the word means much more than just a plain description of that part of the body. A woman only truly possesses a *yoni* when her vulva has become hot and swollen with want, honeyed with readiness.

'When my husband burst in and caught us together it was, without doubt, two *yonis* he saw before him. We were exciting each other in the most compromising fashion – entwined in one of the most complicated and tiring of the ancient Indian female climaxing positions. I was held balanced over her, touching the bed with only one hand and foot. We were pleasuring each other with great, curved-shafted, wooden cocking daggers, plunging the brightly painted phalluses into each other like swords.

'In a fit of rage, my husband went to the Rajah immediately and laid charges against me. In Afmiristan it is thought a terrible crime for two women to lie together. The Rajah was very reluctant to judge me because I was a foreigner, but the laws were very strict on this matter. Given the evidence presented before him he had no choice but to condemn me to the punishment laid down – *santra*, followed by banishment. The only condition he could make was that the sentence should be carried out as secretly as possible, well away from the prying eyes of the Palace.

'That same night, soldiers of the Rajah's private guard came for me. I was spirited away from the capital on horseback and taken to the Rajah's hunting pavilion out on the plains.

'When we arrived there I was prepared for my *santra* in the Rajah's own tent. The soldiers stripped me of my clothes and then tied my hands behind my back. They laid me face down on the carpetted ground and left me there like that, naked and alone.

'There was no light in the tent. For a long time I lay in total darkness. Then, after what seemed like hours, the blackness began to be lifted slightly by a faint orange glow outside the tent. In horror I realised the light was coming from a brazier of coals the soldiers had lit to heat the branding iron that was going to be used on me.

'I could hear one of them blowing the fire with bellows, making it roar and shoot streams of angry sparks up into the air.

'I knew it wouldn't be long now. Can you imagine how scared I felt? My heart was beating so hard it seemed to make my whole body throb. I couldn't breathe properly,

The Pleasure Ring

I was just panting wildly. I was so nervous I couldn't keep still.

'Now this may shock you, but at that time I had my labia lips starched open to increase the pleasure of my lovemaking. My female Afmiri lover had shown me how to do it with a simple little device made from two bent twigs tied together at each end to make a double bow. She'd fitted it into the outer folds of my vulva so that it sprang them right apart and then she'd coated my labia with a special kind of flour paste. When it had dried hard she was able to take the twigs out and leave me fixed open, my lips held back shiny and stiff, my inner flesh drawn out taut. My clitoris was utterly exposed, made into an island surrounded by a crimson lake, permanently presented so that it could be stimulated from any direction, at any time.

'Without even thinking about it I began to squirm my pulled-back pout round and round on the carpet, somehow finding it helped to ease the dreadful tension knotted up inside me. I just lay there doing it more and more, feeling almost sick with fright.

'Suddenly, the tent flap was pulled open and the head jailer came striding into the tent. He was a mighty mountain of a man. In one huge, leather-gloved hand he held aloft the iron rod he'd just plucked from the brazier. The end of it was fiery red; the marking letters glowing brightly in the air.

'He walked over to me and then, without a moment's pause, he brought his arm down and pressed the brand against my thigh.

'For the first single second, I felt no pain. But I was so worked up, so tense with fear that the touch was like a trigger that made every muscle in me jerk in spasm. My whole body went absolutely rigid, arching back, hard and tight all over.

'Amande, I have a secret to tell you.

'You see, even though I hadn't meant it to, constantly rubbing my *yoni* on the carpet had made me very, very ready. You understand what I mean?

'When I threw myself backwards, that moment of uncontrollable convulsion made me thrust my ripe, opened-out sex deep into the harsh wool threads. I was so inflamed, my clitoris was standing out of me like a tiny, red penis. That one massive contraction made me jerk the obscene swelling down into the carpet with unbearable roughness.

'And the awful truth is, Amande, it made me orgasm! I actually came at the very moment they branded me!

'And when the terrible burning pain began it just made it better. The jailer and the soldiers watching all thought that I was screaming and thrashing around in agony. They had no idea that I was almost dying in ecstasy.'

I lie back on the divan with Ladisa's terrible confession echoing round my mind.

And then, something happens to me, happens between my legs. I suddenly feel my vulva go very wet. The juices start to flow inside me and the man's fingers begin to slop between my lips.

He grins and starts to beat me harder. There's nothing I can do to stop him making so much noise. Soon the whole room is filled with the slapping rhythm of my liquid sex being excited.

I hear Ladisa calling out to me weakly, telling me the noise is going to make her come.

I look up at the acrobats. I watch the men reach their climaxes, see their cocks jerk silently as they start to shoot their seed at each other inside the girl.

The Pleasure Ring

I'm going to come too, but it's not looking at them that's going to do it. All I can think of now is Ladisa, sprawled naked in that tent.

I think of her writhing on the carpet in fearful anticipation as the men come in. Think of her bucking back that single, violent time and her smooth, overexcited *yoni* jerking so leathery tight. Think of her tender, raw clitoris rasping savagely into the coarse wool, bringing her instantly to orgasm.

Even worse than this, I begin to imagine myself being taken by her. Being held down against my will in one of the lewd climaxing positions she spoke of. Bent over with my legs forced wide apart, my sex transformed by her into a starch-edged, stretched-back *yoni*, my clitoris completely revealed to her touch. Having to let her bring me to orgasm with an enormous wooden cocking dagger.

How can it be that, though I struggle against it so hard, it is the thought of giving myself up to her in such a perverted way that makes me finally cry out in shuddering climax?

Chapter 22

I've come to an arrangement with Ladisa. Now that I've passed the test at the welcoming entertainment, I'm going to enter preparations for the Ordeal.

We've agreed that if I win at the Trial I will serve my time as Concubine as best I can but, in return, if I lose she will provide me with a berth on a safe ship home to France as soon as possible.

I know that if I were to become the Concubine the customary gifts I will receive would make me a rich woman. But, even so, there is one thing that worries me – I have no idea what Prince Hassan is like.

I know he is reasonably young and reported to be handsome, but I'm really not sure I could endure being his lover for twelve whole months if I wasn't attracted to him at all. Gifts or no gifts.

The only way I'm going to find out anything more about him is by asking Ladisa. The fact that she is so reluctant to talk about him just increases my misgivings.

The only thing I can discover from her is that the other three new competitors are already quartered in rooms similar to mine in distant corners of the palace. El-Marrach is established with her servants in the Concubine's apartments. It has been arranged that we are all kept separated from each other until the competition.

It seems that two of the other girls are whores from Amsterdam who were sailing to the Dutch colonies in search of their fortunes when their ship was captured by pirates.

They were bought from the slave market by Ladisa, but the third woman was actually given to her. She is a wild Irish girl whose past is unclear but who was won by a local merchant in a dice game. She proved to be such a handful the merchant was glad to be rid of her. Ladisa has her under control now, but I can only guess at the methods she's using to do it!

Even though Ladisa visits each of us in turn every day, I can't help feeling that I am her favourite. She seems to spend more time with me than the others and she has told me she intends to supervise my final preparations herself.

It's plain there's no love lost between herself and El-Marrach. She tells me they've crossed swords many times in the past and, apparently, they're not even on speaking terms now. I really believe that, apart from anything else, she's convinced I can beat El-Marrach and that's why she's putting all her efforts behind me.

She comes to my rooms each day to give me lessons about such things as court etiquette and names of all the different important people at the Palace. All things I will have to know if I win the competition. She keeps a close eye on my figure and complexion, making sure I eat well, keeping me out of the sun.

One day when I'm having to parade myself for her, I'm determined to use the opportunity to find out the things I want to know about the Prince.

I'm very devious about it. As I'm posing for her I deliberately distract her attention by letting my dressing robe slip open slightly.

The Pleasure Ring

'Ladisa, I'm worried I might be too tall for the Prince.'

'No, Amande. He's tall too. You're just the right height.'

I smooth my hands down the front of my gown. 'How about my breasts, they're quite large. Does he prefer women with smaller breasts?'

'I'm sure I don't know.'

'And my hair. It's not too short, is it?'

'No. He likes short hair.' A hint of exasperation now.

I twist round and pull the silky robe tight over the cheeks of my buttocks, making it cling to every curve. 'How about my bottom, it's not too big is it?'

Her eyes are on me now. 'Your bottom's fine. You're perfect. The Prince thinks you're beauti . . .'

Her voice trails away, but it's too late. She's said too much.

I spin round to confront her. 'He's seen me, hasn't he? Spied on me somehow. Why didn't you tell me?'

But she's already making for the door, fists clenched in anger at having revealed her master's private affairs so stupidly.

For reasons that I can't sensibly explain I feel ridiculously vexed that Prince Hassan has found some way to view me when I haven't managed to do the same to him.

After Ladisa has left, it begins to eat away at me. I have a bath to take my mind off it, but that doesn't work. Just as I'm getting out of the pool I happen to look out through the shuttered window into the courtyard of what is the servant girls' quarters. There's a line of washing strung across the yard and amongst the clothes is one of the white and purple uniform robes that all the girls wear.

As soon as I see it a plan forms in my mind. With a little effort, I force the shutters fully open. There's no one around. I loosen my dressing gown off and climb up onto the sill. I swing my bare legs out and drop the four or five feet down onto the flagstones below.

It only takes me a few seconds to unpeg the uniform and tie it round me. Lying in the corner, I spy a large stone water jug – the ideal thing to complete my disguise. I lift it up onto my shoulder, using it to hide my face as I steal out into the sunlit passageway.

I've learnt enough of the ways of the Palace to know that at this time of day the Prince will be in his private gardens taking a walk before lunch.

I also know that it is strictly forbidden for anyone to enter there without permission. I dread to think what might happen to me if I'm caught there. But I can't let that change my mind, I have to know what he looks like.

No one pays me a second glance as I hurry along, screened by the pitcher, and it's not long before I arrive at the garden walls. I take a deep breath as I cross through the gateway. I'll have to be much more careful now, stay alert for any movement ahead so that I avoid meeting anybody who might challenge me.

The grounds are arranged in a series of secluded courtyards, linked by pillared arcades. This part of the Palace is even more richly decorated than the rest, every surface embellished with carving and inlays. The plants and flowers are all so beautiful. As I search for the Prince it's like walking through a magical garden.

I hear the sound of water ahead of me and I find myself standing at the edge of a courtyard of trees and flowers where the air is filled with the babble of fountains.

I'm so entranced I lay my jar down and step out into the sunshine to gaze around me.

And then I see him. Standing in the centre of the

The Pleasure Ring

garden, leaning back against the rim of the largest fountain pool.

I'm totally confused. The man I'm looking at is, without a shadow of doubt, the servant who had the task of attending me at the erotic entertainment. I can't understand why he should be here like this, dressed up in what is plainly one of his master's finest robes.

Yet, that is not the most shocking thing. For he is not alone. A naked woman is kneeling in front of him. The servant is resting back with his legs apart, his 'borrowed' robe pulled open and, even from where I'm standing behind her, it is obvious that she is enthusiastically occupied suckling on his heated member.

I'm stunned that the two of them should be taking such a terrible risk, performing an act like this, here in the Prince's own garden, when they must know they could be disturbed by him at any minute. One thing I do know, though, is that I don't want to get caught with them.

I turn to leave as fast as I can, but in my haste, I move too quickly. I see the servant look up and spot me across the courtyard.

For a moment, an expression of annoyance clouds his face, but then I see he recognises me.

With the slightest of movements, he raises his hand to stop my flight and with that single, commanding gesture I realise the trick that he and Ladisa have played on me.

Of course the Prince knows what I look like! He's already arranged the opportunity to stand over me and study me at my most unguarded moment.

Hassan and the servant who brought me to orgasm are one and the same man!

My mouth opens in a silent exclamation of disbelief

and outrage. Then all my anger melts away when I see his handsome face break into a guilty smile.

And now I know that this is Prince Hassan, I realise the woman servicing him so eagerly must be El-Marrach. I look her over with a rival's eye and can't help noticing with a certain envy how thin her rippling body is, how narrow her waist, how shining the long black hair that tumbles down the sinuous smoothness of her flexing back.

It's clear that she has no idea that I'm here and it appears the Prince has no intention of letting her know. He lightly cups one hand behind her head and pulls her closer onto him, impaling her deeper onto his shaft.

Out of sight above her, he begins to signal to me with tiny waves of his fingers. I'm acutely aware of the position I'm in. I've trespassed into the most private part of the Palace and been caught as a voyeur of the Prince's lovemaking. I stand to be severely punished. My only hope is to try and pacify him by doing exactly as he orders.

It is only this that compels me to comply with the totally indecent demands he makes now.

With a flicker of his finger he forces me to take off the stolen uniform. Once it is removed and I'm as bare as El-Marrach, he gestures with his eyes to the side of me. I turn to see he's directing me towards a stone spout that's pouring out a constant arc of water into a small ornamental pool.

At first, I can't believe I've understood his intentions correctly, but a look back at his face tells me I was right. There's no doubt about it. He wants me to hold myself in front of the spout!

Trying to hide my unwillingness, I step over to the pool as he commands. I position myself with my legs placed either side of it and then, hands drawing my labia back

The Pleasure Ring

like curtains, I hesitantly push my hips forward to let the bubbling flow of water play on my clitoris.

The first splash of the tumbling water makes me gasp out. It's only the roar of the fountains that drowns out my cry. The sensation is incredible, like being unendingly stroked by velvet-gloved fingers. It's so unbearable I have to squeeze my lips tight shut to end the torment. Then I open them a second time and take the stimulation until it's too much again. Then I do it again and again until my clitoris has grown erect, has swollen up enough to stand the onslaught.

Now I can hold myself apart and let it ripple and twist between my lips, swirling my clitoris from side to side. I look down at it through the sparkling water and I see it's like a hard, shiny, purple pebble.

I just know doing this to it is going to make me come in some completely new, smooth way, but at the same time, I feel my cheeks flushing red. For a secret shame has come over me. The constant stimulation of the stream is having an altogether different effect, as well. Sending signals up to my bladder. Pulsing, insistent messages I can't ignore. I can feel the want growing inside me all the time, the heaviness pressing down. The burning desire to empty myself.

The signals are getting more urgent. But I can't pull away, I have to try and control myself. I haven't felt like this since I was a little girl. I'm squirming around with the need inside me, knees rubbing together, desperately wanting to cross my legs.

I glance towards Hassan. Does he know what he's doing to me? Am I the first girl he's made stand here like this?

Whatever the truth, watching me now has brought him to the edge of crisis, chest heaving, face contorted, hands resting on El-Marrach's shoulders to support his shaking legs. I know he's waiting, holding back, wanting the sight of my orgasm to bring on his own pleasure.

His eyes order me to do it. I lift onto tiptoes, inching closer to the fountainhead, taking the full force of the flow directly on my nub. I'm in turmoil, unable to restrain the two forces fighting inside me, belly heavy and swollen, clitoris gleaming tight.

The climax comes but, just as I knew it would, it strips away my last desperate attempts to prevent the awful thing happening.

One tiny spurt escapes from me, but that is all it takes to burst the floodgates, to break the strongest taboo. I can't stop now. The most intense feeling of release rushes through my belly and then the warm stream begins to flow out of me. I start to empty my bladder completely, the two rivulets mingling instantly between my legs.

The contractions of orgasm make it pump out of me in gulping jets and I realise this is what it must feel like when a man shoots his sperm. I'm so overcome with embarrassment I have to grasp the spout to support myself. The disgrace of it! The complete humiliation of a grown woman wetting herself like this.

Can Hassan see what I've done? I think I'll die if he can tell.

I hear him groan and look to see him wrenching away from El-Marrach's tonguing caress to display his great, orgasming cock to me.

He shudders and his spunk flies from him, sprinkling onto the scorching, sun-baked stone slabs where it spits and boils as it sizzles away to nothing.

Even though I still feel weak from my own climax, I know I must make my escape now, gather up my clothes and slip away before I'm discovered by El-Marrach.

The Pleasure Ring

Unfortunately for me, she is too experienced not to realise that only something very special would persuade Hassan to deny himself the final ecstasy of spending in her mouth.

Just as I reach the cover of the arcade she tears herself free from his grip and twists round towards me. For that last second our eyes lock in startled recognition.

I should have seen it before! The clue was there before me all the time! Ladisa was wrong.

Her name doesn't refer to the tightness of her vulva. It comes from her French name!

El-Marrach, The Heavenly One.

Angel!

Chapter 23

I don't stop running until I reach the safety of my rooms. There was no mistaking the look of pure hatred that I saw in Angel's face and there's no telling what she'll have Prince Hassan do to me now.

I pace the floor, expecting the Palace guard to come and arrest me at any moment, fearing the approach of every footstep. My only hope is that, somehow, Ladisa will be able to protect me.

The minutes stretch into hours, but still no one comes. It starts to grow cool so I slip under the covers of the bed whilst I wait.

It must be long past midnight when Ladisa arrives. She stands in the doorway looking more angry than I've ever seen before.

'I've just had a very uncomfortable audience with the Prince. He was furious with me. Not only for letting you trick me into revealing that he'd seen you, but also for allowing you to go wandering around the Palace. It's just lucky for both of us he seems to be completely infatuated with you since he saw your performance with the waterspout. He was like a dog on heat every time your name was mentioned.'

I ask anxiously, 'What did El-Marrach say about me?'

'The Prince thought that was very strange. It was obvious

to him that you and she know each other, but when he questioned her about it she denied it. He's sure she's hiding something and so am I. That's partly why I'm here, to find out the truth from you.'

'It's a long story, Ladisa, but if anyone has to hear it, I want it to be you.'

Intrigued, her anger fades now and she crosses over to sit on the side of the bed. For the first time, I begin to tell the full story of my acquaintance with Angelique du Mornay and all the misfortune her trickery has brought down on me. Screened by the darkness I recount every sordid detail of my treatment at her hands.

Ladisa listens in silence, but I could swear I hear her breathing getting heavier as I go on, especially whilst I'm telling her about the time Angel brought me to orgasm with the dildo in Madam Beatrice's cellar. I'm almost sure I feel her fingers secretly playing over the delicious tenderness of her brand marks.

When I've finally finished, though, her mood is more serious. 'No wonder El-Marrach didn't want the Prince to learn any of this. He would be most displeased with her if any of it could be proved against her.

'It does, however, put you in a difficult situation too. You must not, on any account, repeat a word of what you've just told me to anyone else. It is a common occurrence for competitors in the Ordeal to try and discredit their rivals.

'I believe you, but you have no real evidence that what you say is true. The Prince would not listen to your accusations, particularly when they're aimed against the present Concubine. It may well turn him against you. I have ways of using such information, but you must keep absolutely quiet.'

She stands up slowly.

The Pleasure Ring

'Despite what you've told me, I regret we must now come to the second part of my reason for visiting. You must prepare yourself for bad news.'

She pauses dramatically, deliberately keeping me in nervous suspense.

'El-Marrach has used her influence to demand that you are punished for your impudent trespassing. The Prince has been forced to instruct me to carry out the sentence tonight.'

'What is my punishment to be?' I ask, fearing the worst.

'I have been ordered to give you a severe lashing, at least a hundred strokes.'

From the depths of her robes she produces an evil-looking flogging whip. I quake as she flicks it at me menacingly, only to be unsettled more when she lets it drop onto the bed and begins to slowly unwind the folds of her robes instead.

'It's just lucky for you that the Prince never specified what I was to lash you with or where the strokes were to be applied. It means we have one very different option open to us.'

I'm scandalised. 'You don't mean . . . ?'

'Yes, my dear, I'm afraid I do. But don't think you'll be getting off lightly. You're going to be surprised just how much torture I can inflict with this tongue of mine!'

She slides in beside me under the sheets, skin-janglingly naked. I immediately turn my back on her in a show of resistance, but can still feel the hardness of her nipples pressing into my back, the softness of her thighs against the back of my legs. And there's no escape from the musky warmth of her perfume.

Accepting my reluctance, she begins gently. Doing no

more than just stroking her fingers through my hair, she whispers in the darkness, 'You know I couldn't help being excited by your story. Especially when I knew I was going to give you this punishment as soon as you'd finished. Feel what you've done to me.' She pushes herself forward, making her sex touch against my buttocks, smearing her dampness against me.

'Maybe I should tell you a story now. Make you as excited as you were when I told you about my branding. Shall I tell you about the way I was brought to my first orgasm and the woman who so cleverly arranged to be the one who did it?

'I was just sixteen at the time. It happened that my parents had to go away for the summer and, because I was too young to be left on my own, they sent me to stay with a friend of my mother. This woman, Anne, lived in a remote cottage out in the woods. There were only the two of us, but we got on very well. We talked a lot, though I found the way she continually brought the subject round to boys and my feelings about them embarrassing. I think right from the start she'd guessed that I wasn't interested in them at all and was trying to get me to admit I liked girls more.

'There were two bedrooms upstairs in her cottage. Anne's was the first on the landing and mine the second. It meant I always had to pass her door to get to mine. One evening, after I'd been there only a few nights, we were sitting downstairs together when Anne announced she was feeling tired and was going to bed early. She went up to her room and left me downstairs alone.

'Much later, when I went to bed myself, I tried very hard not to wake her. I didn't take a candle with me, feeling my way up the stairs in the darkness. When I reached the

The Pleasure Ring

landing I couldn't help noticing her door had been left half open. I was surprised she still had her candle burning and it was impossible to resist looking through the doorway as I crept past.

'I discovered I could see across her room to her dressing table where her mirror was standing. The shocking thing was I could see Anne reflected in it, moving around on the bed out of sight behind the door.

'She was lying on top of the covers with no clothes on, stroking up and down between her legs with her hairbrush. I could see her face, drawn into a look of concentration and agitation that I didn't fully understand. After a little while she began to roll about, then suddenly something happened to her and she jerked forward and then sighed and fell back weakly.

'I hurried on to my own room, greatly disturbed by what I'd seen. Until that moment I'd never really understood what sexual pleasure was. Now I'd watched her having what I knew must be an orgasm, the mixture of horror and fascination I felt about it was so strong it made me feel sick inside.

'That night I kept going over and over in my head what I'd seen and I couldn't stop thinking about it the next morning, either. When Anne told me after lunch that she was going out for a walk, I knew I had to make some excuse to stay behind.

'As soon as she'd gone, I ran upstairs to my room and took all my clothes off. Clutching my hand to my quim in the utmost state of excitement, I tiptoed, naked, from my room along the landing to Anne's. Feeling like a thief I searched through her drawers until I found the brush I'd seen her with. I needed to know what it felt like so badly that I started to stroke it against my strangely hot sex, then and there, just like I'd seen her doing.

'I began to sweep the soft, fine hairs up and down and it did things to me I'd never felt before. And the more I did it the better it got. I started to work the brush harder and harder. I could feel my heart pounding, my legs shaking. It got so good I just knew I was close to the sighing time that I'd seen Anne have. But I just couldn't quite reach it. I was teetering on the edge of something wonderful, but I didn't know what I was looking for, didn't know how to get there. You can imagine the state I was getting into. Rubbing myself frantically, almost in tears now.

'I was so distraught that I didn't hear Anne coming up the stairs. I had no idea she was there until she threw the bedroom door open and caught me red-handed, standing there with my legs apart and her best brush pressed into my damp quim.

'Of course, it never occurred to me at the time that I'd been led into a trap. The leaving of her door ajar, the positioning of her mirror, were all carefully planned. Anne wanted me to see her because she knew I wouldn't be able to resist the temptation she'd laid in front of me. Now, under cover of her outrage, she knew she had the power she needed to force me into answering her questions. Pretending to be controlling her anger, she wagged her finger at me. "You're in a lot of trouble, young lady. Don't even try to deny what you were doing!"

'"I'm sorry, Anne. I . . . I . . ."

'"How many times have you used my brush to masturbate with?"

'"Never before. I swear it. This was the first time."

'Now we came to it.

'"I suppose you use your fingers usually, do you?"

The Pleasure Ring

'No answer.

'"But you have come before? You have had an orgasm, haven't you?"

'I shook my head this time, my ears burning at her words.

'"Well, don't worry, that won't be a problem when I've finished with you. You've been caught doing wrong and I intend to teach you a lesson you'll never forget."

'I was too afraid to protest when she told me to go and stand in the corner like some naughty schoolgirl, making me wait there whilst she went to fetch the things she needed. She ordered me not to even think of touching myself whilst she was away, but it was very difficult. Even now I can remember the feeling of dread that engulfed me, the sure knowledge that she was going to come back and do something to me that was so terrible, yet so incredibly exciting, I couldn't even begin to imagine it. I stood there jigging from foot to foot, squeezing my legs together, making my quim lips roll up and down between my thighs. I'm sure I would have had my first orgasm like that if Anne hadn't arrived back so soon.'

Ladisa pauses. All the time she's been speaking she's been massaging her hands along my back, breaking down my defences, weakening my resolve. And now she's taken me too far. I don't want her to stop. I hear myself saying, 'Go on! Tell me more!'

Victory is hers. I'm forced to surrender the fortress of my sex to her invading fingers before she will continue.

'When she returned she called me out of the corner and marched me along the landing to my own room. She was carrying some short lengths of rope and something else in a bag that she wouldn't let me see. She ordered me to lie on the bed and then tied my hands and feet to the bedposts.

She tied my legs out very wide, but even then she took one of the pillows and forced it under my buttocks so that my thighs were stretched farther apart still. She lifted me up so that my quim was pushing right out of me.

'And then, when I was completely restrained, she brought the hidden thing out.

'It was a bunch of young, green nettles!

'I couldn't believe what she was planning to do, but it was true!

'Totally ignoring all my pleading and crying, she began to draw the stems down very lightly over my quim. She did it slowly so that the stings came one after another with little breaks in between, so that each one made me buck and jerk afresh. She was very thorough. She made sure the needle-fine barbs pierced me everywhere, on my outer lips, on my labia, and especially on my clitoris.

'And then, she left me. Just went out and closed the door behind her.

'I was in agony. The pain of the stings got worse and worse. I lay there screaming, calling out to her to take mercy on me, to let me free so that I could do something to ease the terrible burning.

'Hours passed, darkness came and still she did not return. I began to feel tired, but I couldn't sleep. My quim was on fire. I couldn't lie still. I kept twisting and turning, vainly trying to gain some relief by massaging my thighs together.

'I was left like that the whole night long. I didn't sleep at all. I ached to scratch the terrible itching between my legs. By morning, I was exhausted.

'My only solace was that the burning had subsided now, mellowed into a prickly smarting. But when I looked down I could see that my quim had swollen up severely overnight.

The Pleasure Ring

It bulged out of me, pink and inflamed. I couldn't bear for my thighs to even touch against it now.

'It was just after dawn that Anne came back. She knew exactly when the right time was going to be. I could see she hadn't slept much either. She had the hairbrush with her.

'She told me not to speak. She simply said, "Prepare yourself for your initiation!" and then she touched me with the brush and I nearly passed out.

'My quim seemed to explode with sensation. It was so tender, so responsive, glowing with excitement shot through with darting arrows of pure white pain. As she began to stroke the brush over me I moaned out to her, first begging her to stop and then begging her not to. I was on fire in a different way now.

'She quickly took me to the place I'd reached the afternoon before. I could feel the same tightness building up inside me again. The same desperation.

'But this time Anne had prepared me. She'd weakened my mind with tiredness overnight, and now she was overwhelming my body with waves of conflicting emotions. I was frightened by what I was feeling, but the tingling sharpness of the nettle stings kept robbing me of control, made it so hard to contain the ball of pleasure I could feel in the pit of my stomach, growing bigger and stronger all the time.

'I started to call out to her that it was too much, that I couldn't bear it any longer.

'But she just shouted back, "This is what I've longed to do to you ever since you got here. There's no going back now. I'm going to do it all the way. Don't struggle against it. You know it's what you need!"

'And now a new feeling began to erupt inside me. One that I couldn't stop, one that made me shake and convulse.

It took me over, filled me with such exquisite pain that all I could do was sob out, "Please. Oh please! Something's happening to me. I can't stand it. Stop. Please stop. You're breaking something inside me!"

'But she carried on stroking me. She made the terrible thing happen and I screamed as it wracked my body. And as I thrashed on the bed in rapture she took me in her arms and comforted me. "It's alright, my darling. It's alright. It's meant to be like this. You're there, you're coming!"

Now, her story ended, I feel Ladisa moving behind me, drawing herself up onto all fours. She begins to kiss across my shoulders, gently but firmly, pressing me over onto my back. She whispers, 'I'm going to do my duty now,' and she begins to bury herself under the sheets, worming her way down the bed. Her hands find my ankles and pull them apart. I lie with my legs spread open, allowing her to slip between them. Curled up there she is no more than a rounded hump in the bedclothes.

I feel her fingers running up my inner thighs. She slides them either side of my sex and pulls it apart, stretching the hood of my clitoris right back. I stare at the ceiling in shamefilled dismay. I've never, ever even dreamt of letting another woman . . . you know, lick me, before, yet here I am offering myself without a struggle, allowing Ladisa to do exactly as she wishes.

I feel totally inhibited. I lie rigid on the mattress like a Y-shaped piece of wood and can sense her head moving forward. Unexpectedly, she blows on my exposed nub and the coolness of her breath makes me shudder all over. I'm so incredibly hot! Maybe I really want this more than I'm willing to admit, even to myself.

Then she touches the tip of her tongue to my quim and I groan involuntarily. She sinks her mouth on me and starts

The Pleasure Ring

kissing and, try as I might, I can't pretend I don't like what she's doing. Her tongue is lapping so gently, just skimming my clitoris. It's not long before my legs relax and my knees bend up, letting her in farther between my thighs. My back arches up to angle my hips forward to meet her mouth. I start to run my fingers through my hair.

I'm disgustingly wet now; lifting up and down on the bed, rocking my sex against her face. It's been so easy for her to do this to me. I'm going to come soon. Very soon.

It's just as the first ripples of orgasm begin to spread through me that I see the door opening.

A man enters – Prince Hassan!

I freeze, motionless. I glimpse his face in the moonlight for just a second as he steps into the room, but how much I see written in that expression!

I see he truly has fallen for me. That he's been lying awake, unable to sleep for thinking about me. That his desire has driven him to my door in the middle of the night, expecting to find me recovering tearfully from the lashing he sentenced me to and now regrets. He's even brought a jar of some sort of soothing lotion with him as an excuse for his visit. In his mind he sees me hesitantly allowing him to uncover my reddened buttocks so that he can tenderly apply the lotion to them. And when he has me in his hands, massage will turn naturally to caress, caress to passionate embrace and then, just as night follows day, that embrace will turn to such sultry, bed-creaking coupling that it will wake all the servant girls and they'll lie there, fingering themselves enviously as they listen to us. All this I see in that moment.

Already the thought of it has raised his ardour. In his haste to cross over to the bed he accidentally allows his robe to fall open to reveal that most awkward of things for men to conceal – an erect penis, standing rampant with anticipation.

But as he nears the bed his face changes when he sees the dune of sheets between my legs.

Ladisa is still there, oblivious to what is happening. Of all the nights, of all the times he could have come to me, why did it have to be tonight? Why did he have to discover me like this? What must he think of me?

He takes hold of a corner of the covers and rips them off the bed. He must know already what he is going to find, but it still makes him gasp.

He discovers me with my legs spread open wide, with Ladisa's wet face pressed deep into my sex. She breaks away from me in shock, but Hassan's hands move quickly to her raised buttocks and hold her in place. He addresses her harshly, speaking in French. For my benefit, I've no doubt.

'Stay there, Ladisa. If this is how you think my orders should be carried out then it is only right that you should take your own punishment in the same manner!'

He pushes her forward roughly, squeezing her mouth back against my sex as he tears his robe open. He positions himself directly behind her at the end of the bed and lifts the tip of his cock to the valley of her backward facing pout. Ladisa's excitement at seducing me is her downfall now. She's turned her own sex into a *yoni* and he's able to slide his shaft into her with ease.

I wonder how long it is since she last had a man inside her? How much she must hate it!

What a tangle of dark emotions is woven between us now!

I, distraught at being discovered fornicating this way.

The Pleasure Ring

Ladisa forced to submit to an act with Hassan that is as unnatural to her as her tonguing is to me.

And the Prince himself, here in my room, presented with two wet vulvas, only to find that, through pride, he must deny himself the one he lusts after so strongly and force himself upon the other that offers him no welcome.

He rides into Ladisa hard, spite and jealousy spurring him on. And every time he plunges into her he jolts her face forward into my sex, making her lips grind against me.

His left hand is round under her belly now, strumming her clitoris with feverish fingers. But his right hand finds her most sacred place. He lets his fingers trace over the raw weal of her brand, exploring the ridges and peaks of it with probing fingertips. I feel her tensing, unable to deny her arousal at this dual caress.

She does not suffer alone, though. In the throes of her own excitement she pulls my clitoris deep into her mouth and gnaws and sucks on it distractedly. I call out wildly, begging her to finish me.

But Hassan denies me cruelly. He tears Ladisa away from me, pulling her shoulders back towards him to clasp her kneeling limply upright in the darkness. He holds her up silhouetted in front of me, displaying her to me as he enters her urgently, wanting to show me how he would have taken me.

There is also one further humiliation he intends to make Ladisa suffer for her disobedience. He drops his arms to her sex and cups it in both hands. He begins to rub his palms vigorously, like he was warming his hands together on a winter's morning, trapping her between them.

I see her biting her lip, desperate not to give him the pleasure of hearing her making noise. His hands work faster and faster. He must be making her so very hot and red. She tries to fight against it, but it's no use. No woman could help herself, being rubbed like that. Her head lolls forward and she starts to come, shattered at having been masturbated to orgasm against her will.

Hassan shows her no pity as she suffers the climax. His thighs smack against her buttocks as he forces himself into her clenching tightness to bring himself release. It's only moments before his cock begins to vent.

How deeply he stares into my eyes as he starts to fill Ladisa with the spunk that we both know was meant for me!

I feel my clitoris throbbing. I yearn to touch myself, but I resist. I want to show him what he's missing too. I grip my hands through the slats of the bed head and hold on for dear life. There's no stopping it now. I feel the spasms building up inside me, feel them coming faster and faster. My throbbing clitoris quivers in the open air between my spread legs. Then, suddenly, it goes stiff and I orgasm spontaneously and Hassan calls out my name as I start to writhe sensuously in the wet pool of my own juices.

Chapter 24

I feel deeply despondent the next morning. I begin to realise just how attracted I am to Hassan myself. I keep thinking how he looked last night, how sexily his body moved in the darkness as he took Ladisa so vigorously. And now, because of what's happened, I'm absolutely sure he won't even allow me to be a competitor at the Ordeal.

Knowing he's ordered Ladisa to go to him before she visits me, I'm fully prepared for bad news when she arrives.

You can imagine my happiness when I discover she has been sent on a different kind of errand altogether. For Hassan has dispatched her to me with flowers and a note that simply reads 'Sorry'.

I feel like shouting for joy. My future plans are clear to me now. I'm going to dedicate myself to winning the Ordeal. Not only so that I can become Hassan's concubine, but also so that I can take my vengeance on Angel by depriving her of all she desires.

Even though I should only officially enter my period of preparation in a fortnight's time, I tell Ladisa I want to start straight away. I want to train harder and push myself farther than all the others.

Pleased with my new-found commitment, she readily agrees to my plan. She tells me I can begin that very afternoon – by having my sex shaved as the rules of the competition demand!

When she returns later, she spreads a cloth over the low table and makes me lie back over it. I have to open my legs as wide as possible whilst she stipples all over between my thighs with a soap-lathered brush. There's nothing too bad about that, it's the thin-bladed shaving knife that makes me really nervous. I see it flashing in the light as she strops the delicate arc of steel to wicked sharpness. It's only my absolute determination to triumph in the Ordeal that holds me down on the table.

I'm so tense, I have to shut my eyes as she turns to start. I jump ridiculously when the cold metal touches me the first time but, after that, it's surprisingly easy. She works deftly, quickly shaving away my tangled triangle of hair before moving on downwards. I hold my breath as she pulls and tugs me this way and that, razoring over my most delicate parts.

Only after she's buffed me over with a pumice stone and dusted me with scented powder does she allow me to explore what she has done to me. I can't believe how different I feel, so smooth and soft. This is the first time I've ever been like this, but I really like it. It makes my vulva feel so sensitive, so much more sexual. I'm aware of it all the time. When I put my robe back on it seems to glide backwards and forwards over it as I walk around. I feel like I've got a hot little volcano between my legs, the bare outer slopes of my mound rising out of me up to the fiery crater.

But, as Ladisa reminds me, I'm going to have little time to enjoy this new sensation. As the second part of my preparations she intends to start my beatings tonight. This afternoon will be my last opportunity to orgasm until the

The Pleasure Ring

Ordeal and she suggests that I make full use of the few hours left to me to relieve myself fully before my enforced abstinence begins.

A little coyly, she presents me with a book she's brought to help me in this task. It's an illustrated erotic manuscript that she's borrowed from Quisic-al-Rashid, Prince Hassan's tutor in all matters sexual and a man I will meet intimately during the Ordeal itself.

I know shaving me has excited Ladisa and I'm sure she secretly hopes that I will look at the book whilst she's there. She can't hide her disappointment when I pointedly put it to one side until she has, very reluctantly, left.

As soon as she's gone, though, I lock the door and eagerly lounge back on the cushioned divan with the book in front of me. I lift one leg a little to open my robe to the waist, wanting to let the cool air soothe the tingling in my newly exposed flesh.

I open the book to find it filled with the most beautiful paintings. But they are all flagrantly pornographic, page after page showing scenes of the most lecherous couplings.

It happens that I already know the story from Ladisa. The pictures tell the tale of a licentious youth who is the apprentice of a certain caliph's sorcerer. The young man has already learnt a little of his master's magic and puts it to use with aphrodisiac potions that he sprinkles onto the vulvas of the eager, dusky whores at the local brothel. He's shown amongst the rich decorations of their rooms, copulating with them in many difficult and athletic positions, their sexes swollen to awesome size by the stimulating powders. The women are identified as whores by their silver jewellery. In Pernia only prostitutes wear ankle and wrist bangles and have their noses and ears pierced with rings. The bangles have tiny bells on them that ring louder and louder and faster and faster as the girls are ridden to climax.

The youth notices that his master has started to sleep during the day and then, mysteriously, leave the house unseen at night-time. Curious, he stays awake and spies on the sorcerer from another room. He sees him take a cloak from out of a hidden chest and, to his great astonishment, when the sorcerer slips it over his shoulders he becomes invisible!

The youth sees the door appear to open by itself and then close quietly again. He realises the sorcerer has gone out and, using his limited powers, he conjures up the power of second sight to follow him through the streets.

The caliph has a beautiful young daughter and it is well known that he is so concerned to protect her chastity he keeps her locked under guard at night-time. No man is supposed to be allowed near her, but the apprentice watches the concealed sorcerer calmly walk past all her guards and make his way to her bedroom. He disturbs her masturbating excitedly on the bed in anticipation of his nightly visit.

Still under his cloak of invisibility, the sorcerer throws himself upon her and proceeds to fondle and ravish her. The apprentice is treated to the vision of the princess writhing naked on the bed, seemingly alone, yet thrusting her hips up and down with the utmost lewdness as if she was being powerfully mounted. The innocent, but willing girl quickly arrives at orgasm as she is despoiled once again by the unseen genie who comes to her night after night and teaches her all manner of delightful and previously unthought of acts of pleasure.

Seeing how beautiful she truly is, the apprentice vows

The Pleasure Ring

that he must have her as well. The very next morning he steals the cloak from its concealed place whilst the sorcerer sleeps. He dons it himself and goes out in search of the princess.

He discovers her with a party of other young ladies of the court, bathing at a secluded pool. A dozen naked girls parade themselves for him unwittingly, but he only has eyes for the princess. He draws near her whilst she dries herself and touches his hand on her shoulder. She is startled but, believing it is her secret spirit lover, she quickly recovers herself and daringly allows him to arrange her towel wrap so that her buttocks are only half covered at the rear.

On the way back to the palace the apprentice places himself behind her and gains entry to her as she walks along the path with her friends. The princess has the utmost difficulty in disguising her arousal as she's taken this way, having to try and walk normally whilst the invisible cock is thrust in and out of her.

Unfortunately, as they pass through an olive grove, the cloak becomes snagged on a low branch and, unbeknown to the apprentice, it is pulled off his shoulders. You can imagine the scene when the other girls turn round to find the two of them mated together so rudely in full view of them all.

It takes the sorcerer's strongest spells and all of his powers to set everything back to rights. He knows full well that his own activities will be found out if he does not. However, once he has blown a thick mist of forgetfulness over all those concerned, he turns his attention back to the apprentice and casts an awful spell on him as a punishment.

He changes his body round so that his anus and penis are exchanged in position. He transforms him so that he is left with his tight little puckered hole between his legs like a virgin's sex and his member standing out from the cheeks of his buttocks like a tongue from a mouth. As the final cruelty, he not only sentences the youth to continual, lustful erection but also condemns him to remain like that until he has made love to a man as a woman and to a woman as a man.

When the apprentice looks at himself in a mirror, he finds to his horror that his penis has become grossly erect. And there's nothing he can do to ease it. No matter how often he brings himself off, his lusting stiffness will not subside.

He's forced to wear a special kind of wicker cage under his clothes. One that covers his whole bottom, not only to disguise his deformity, but also to protect his shiny cockhead from the constant rubbing of his robes.

He returns to the brothel, burning with desire, but when he reveals himself to the women there they will not let him enter them for fear of becoming enchanted as well.

Humiliatingly, they will only consent to massaging him to spurting release by fixing a leather collar round his foreskin and jiggling it up and down on the end of a long stick.

In his desperation to recapture the sensation of entering a woman again he's reduced to tying two silk pillows together and, holding them against his buttocks, forcing his cock in and out between them. He's shown at the moment of climax, bent over with the tip of his mauve penis pushing out the other side of the cushions, jetting floods of white semen out behind him.

Eventually, the whores at the brothel take pity on him and offer to help him fulfil the conditions the sorcerer has set him. They bring him into the brothel and dress him as a woman, painting his face with make-up, ornamenting him with the bangles, rings and chains that are their trademark.

The Pleasure Ring

They lubricate the pursed entrance of his forbidden passage that now lies in the same place as their own sex and then they arrange him on a divan couch in a dimly lit bedroom, instructing him to wait there until a suitable client arrives.

Later that night four drunken soldiers lurch into the brothel demanding to be serviced. The whores select the most intoxicated one and guide him through to the back room. In his stupor the soldier falls upon the reclining apprentice and, hoisting the youth's robes up to his waist, inserts his ready member without delay. The whores, anxiously listening with their ears pressed to the other side of the door, hear the apprentice's loud moans as the clenched ring of his anus is violated for the first time.

They hear the soldier gasp at the tightness he finds within, closer and narrower even than any virgin he has known before. He thrusts into the apprentice with unrestrained desire and quickly reaches a frenzied orgasm.

The apprentice's suffering is not over yet, though. For the soldier takes it into his head to share his wonderful discovery with his three friends. He calls them into the room and then locks the door behind them. The whores gather round, laughing and joking as they listen to the apprentice's cries and the sound of the bells on his bangles being jingled vigorously again and again throughout the night.

Some days later, when the apprentice has finally recovered from his ordeal, the whores bring him good news. Their lusty young noblemen clients are full of gossip concerning a rich merchant of the city who has recently taken a young bride even though he is an old man. The rumour from his servants is that she has now found he is unable to perform his duties as a husband and the noblemen are all laying wagers as to who will be the first amongst them to be able to tempt her into their own beds. The resourceful apprentice sees an excellent opportunity to take advantage of the situation.

He gains access to the merchant's household by taking a job as a kitchen boy and soon learns that once a week the merchant and his young wife dine together in the main room of the house. On the night of their next dinner, the youth arranges to have false messages delivered to both of them.

The note delivered to the merchant's wife pretends to be from her husband. It informs her that he has arranged a special surprise for her that night, but that modesty and his own feeling of shame force him to plead with her not to make any sign or mention of it to him during the meal.

The second message delivered to the merchant himself pretends, in turn, to come from his wife, telling him that she is embarrassed to relate that she has been stung by a bee in the most intimate of places. Due to the severity of the swelling she will be obliged to sit on a special soft-cushioned stool at the meal that night. She would be very grateful if her husband would spare her blushes and not make any mention of her condition, nor draw any attention to her discomforted movement during the meal.

With his scheme set in motion, all that remains to be done is for the apprentice to conceal himself at the wife's end of the table that night. He kneels on all fours facing away from the table, resting over a low wooden milking stool positioned amongst the other cushioned seats. He disguises himself with a tapestry throw with a hole cut in it that allows his member to poke through into the open air. As he settles down over the stool, his exposed cock swings up to point skywards from out of his covered buttocks. For the final touch, he reaches round

The Pleasure Ring

and drapes a light cloth over the rolled-back pillar of his erection.

The young bride arrives first and when she sees her new 'seat' she realises immediately that this is the surprise her husband has promised her. She lifts the cloth away excitedly and you can imagine her delight when she reveals what is below it!

Deciding that the stool and its enticing attachment must be some wonderful mechanical device that her husband has brought back from his travels, she feels her sex growing moist with anticipation. But she remembers the words of her husband's note. When he arrives she says nothing, just hitches up her gown discreetly at the moment she sits down and, stifling a groan of pleasure, impales herself gratefully upon the full length of the seat's so-lifelike shaft.

And once she is pressed home she is astonished to feel the seat begins to move beneath her, probing the shaft in and out of her sex. As the meal begins, she tries to remain as demure as she can for her husband's sake, but the stimulation of riding on the seat makes it harder and harder all the time. She longs for an opportunity to slip her hand below the table so that she can furtively finger herself to release.

The merchant observes his wife wriggling and twisting on her peculiar cushioned seat but, recalling her note, he feels sympathy for her and remains silent too. As the meal goes on he sees her face flushing redder and redder and realises she is suffering terribly. It occurs to him that she must be desperate to scratch the dreadful itching of the bee's sting. Searching to give her a polite way out of her dilemma, he pretends to drop into a doze.

Seeing his eyes close, his wife indeed seizes the moment offered, though to rub herself in a very different way than the merchant imagines. Her fingers dive under her gown and go straight to her throbbing clitoris. Under the throw, the apprentice senses her nearing pleasure and begins to buck against her all the faster. His movements quickly bring the frustrated young woman to silent, but delirious, orgasm and as she climaxes she's amazed to feel the pole of the incredible contraption begin to pump and squirt inside her in the most realistic way.

Having now completed his two trials, the youth returns to the sorcerer the next day and demands to be returned to his old self. When his former master hears the tale of how his tasks were fulfilled he is so amused by the youth's ingenuity that he willingly reverses the spell and, forgiving him everything, takes him back as his pupil.

Some of the pictures in the book are really scandalous. I'm sure that when the apprentice is being ridden by the soldiers in the brothel you can see come running out of his reversed cock and dripping down the side of the bed!

I come more times than I can count. By the time Ladisa returns with the stinging lotion and the paddle, she finds me lying languidly on the divan, completely satiated. I can tell she's piqued that I've pleasured myself so thoroughly without letting her share any of the enjoyment.

She orders me to sit me on the edge of the bed in a very cold manner. And, when she starts to beat the paddle against me, I'm sure there's more than a little spite in the way she lays the strokes on me so firmly.

Chapter 25

The days to the Ordeal pass slowly in an endless routine of exercising, bathing and sleeping. I feel really fit but, by the end of the last week, I'm getting very, very frustrated. Now, I almost wish I hadn't read Quisic's book before I started my preparations. The pictures come into my mind all the time. I keep fantasising about winning the competition and Prince Hassan making love to me in the way the apprentice was doing to one of the whores at the beginning of the story. He'd made her do a handstand with her back against a wall and he was holding her up by her feet, drilling his cock down into her upturned sex and making her come upside down. The thing that really excited me about it was the flushed red expression on the whore's face. When you hold the book one way up it looks as if she is suffering from the exertion of the position, but, when you reverse it, it looks as though she is almost expiring from sexual rapture. I can't wait to find out for myself which is the truth!

Ladisa is a tower of strength in these last days. I don't think I could have got this far without her support. I'm more convinced than ever that she is doing everything she can to make sure I win. And when the Ordeal finally begins she proves it to me.

The arrangements for the trials are simple. Each evening for five days, one of the competitors is taken to a special room in the Palace and orgasmed to exhaustion by Quisic in front of witnesses. Ladisa is allowed to decide the order in which the new contenders attend the Ordeal but, as the present Chief Concubine, Angel has the right to go last.

Ladisa has placed one of the Dutch whores first in line, followed by the Irish girl and then the second Dutch whore. I will undergo the Ordeal on the day before Angel.

It is the second evening now. The first whore is back in her rooms recovering from what Quisic put her through. I don't know how well she did and Ladisa hasn't told me yet. Though as she put her first, I can only guess that Ladisa considered her the weakest of us.

Ladisa has told me over and over again that I must try to get as much rest as I can, so I'm a little surprised when she arrives at my door unexpectedly, just as I'm preparing for bed. Even more so when I observe that, even though it's a dark night, she has no candlelight and she's swathed in a dark cloak.

She slips into my room, holding her finger to her lips to keep me silent until the door is safely closed behind her. Drawing me close, she confesses that she's so keen that I do well in my Ordeal tomorrow, she's willing to break all the rules. She's going to take me to a secret viewing place that looks out into the room where the Irish girl is going to be climaxed tonight. I will be able to watch and learn so that I'll be all the better prepared for my own trial at Quisic's hands in two days' time. Producing a second cloak, she wraps it round me and, together, we melt out into the black night like phantoms.

We hug the shadows until we arrive in a windowless courtyard. In the very corner there's a wooden hatchway set into the ground. I help Ladisa to pull it open and a set of stone steps is revealed. She gestures me ahead of her

The Pleasure Ring

and I go down into some kind of disused cellar. When she closes the door behind us the room is thrown into total darkness, except for two honeycombs of light that shine in from grilles set up high in the far wall. Ladisa goes to look through one and I peer through the other.

I find myself looking out across the Orgasming Room at floor level. It's a circular arena, sunk into the centre of a bigger room, surrounded by a wall of about breast height. Beyond the wall the floor rises up steeply in tiers, like a theatre. I'm shocked to see that all the levels are full of Pernian men, sitting or half lying on couches, smoking hookah pipes and waiting with glazed eyes. The smoky air is heavy with the scent of hashish.

For some reason I'd assumed that when Ladisa had said there would be witnesses she meant two or three trustworthy courtiers – not a hundred or so salacious onlookers. I scan the rows of faces, but there is no sign of Hassan.

In the middle of the arena, a flat woven mattress has been laid on the floor. Candles burn in holders stationed at each corner and in the centre a single triangular red silk cushion has been carefully positioned. Ladisa whispers to me that this special hard pillow is a *hi-jin*, a masturbation saddle.

After a few moments the crowd stirs as Quisic enters the arena. He bows politely and then walks over to a black door. He throws it open and beckons the Irish girl into the arena from her waiting room.

A tall, slim, black-haired beauty emerges into the ring and crosses confidently over to the mattress. As she walks she cups her full breasts to stop them swaying, but deliberately leaves her hairless sex on full view.

There's an audible gasp from the men. The girl has had

the whole of her mound tattooed. The dark blue pagan design shows some kind of mythical serpent coiled and knotted round her vulva, its forked tongue lapping at her clitoris. The girl smiles to herself at the stir she's caused, used to the effect her body decoration has on every man who sees it.

Quisic helps her to lie down on the mattress, face towards the floor, carefully positioning her beautified sex directly over the *hi-jin*. I can hear the men talking and, even though I can't understand what they're saying, I know they're discussing the shape of her body, the length of her legs, the pale split of her decorated quim; all so different from their own wives and lovers.

Quisic lights a brass incense burner and places it next to the girl's sideways-turned face, positioning it in such a way that she can't help breathing in the white smoke that drifts out of it. Ladisa whispers to me, 'Opium. Very strong. He'll put it on her quim now too.'

I see Quisic move round to the other end of the mat carrying a brush in a delicate pottery bowl. He kneels between her legs and gently parts her ankles, opening her up so that he can paint the inside folds of her vulva with the syrupy stimulant mixture from the bowl.

It seems to take effect straight away. As soon as he's begun, the girl starts to slither wantonly against the pillow.

When he's coated her all over he places the bowl behind him and starts to massage her. He moves up and down her body rubbing and kneading her expertly, relaxing every part of her except for her pulsing sex, making her moan with desire.

She keeps inhaling the smoke from the burner, taking it in deeper now. I sense that it's nearly time for the Ordeal to begin.

The Pleasure Ring

He lets her drift sensuously until he knows she's completely ready and then he moves his hands up to cup her buttocks in both hands. He begins to rock her backwards and forwards over the cushion, making her sex spread open across it so that her honeyed lips graze against the shiny silk cover again and again. After all these days of abstinence her clitoris must be so, so sensitive to being excited like that. I hardly dare think what it will do to me when my turn comes.

I hear the rising clamour of the men's voices, see them throwing down coins onto the tables. And suddenly I realise what they're doing. They're gambling! They're all making bets with each other on the number of times the girl's going to orgasm!

And the first one doesn't take long in coming. Quisic keeps rocking her firmly and steadily, bringing her gently to the edge and then taking her into the orgasm straight away. She actually screams in pleasure when she comes, but he just calmly calls out aloud, 'The first,' in Arabic.

His hands never stop moving and, dispassionately, he works her up to the same state almost immediately. Calling out the count again, he climaxes her for the second time.

After that, the orgasms start to flow effortlessly. In her drugged haze they seem to wash over her like breaking waves. I see her slipping away, drifting down beneath them, overwhelmed by their power. Even though it's plain she's not aware of what's happening anymore, the men keep roaring at her, urging her on. Her back is shiny with perspiration. I hear Quisic counting higher and higher. Her body goes slack, but still he continues rubbing her over the pillow, forcing more and more orgasms out of her. Her comings are no more than faint sighs and wincing jerks now, so very different from her first gut-wrenching explosions.

At last she's spent. Quisic rests his hands and the girl's body droops with exhaustion.

He lets her sink into oblivious sleep, but he stays beside her. The crowd start to shout again. After a few moments he lifts his hand to quiet them and then pulls out a rope of green jade beads from a pocket in his robe. There are maybe seven or eight of them, each the size of an olive, tied in a string with little gaps in between them. He dips his fingers into the bowl of syrup and uses them to thoroughly lubricate the girl's undefended anus. Then he begins to feed the beads into her, one after the other, until they've all disappeared and only the tasselled end of the cord remains.

I turn to Ladisa anxiously. She confides in a quiet voice, 'The Dutch whore came much more than that last night. The Irish girl's out of the competition already. Now the men in the crowd want Quisic to entertain them by using her to give a demonstration of his sexual prowess. The girl's so drugged she won't remember a thing about this tomorrow morning. They never do! I'm afraid it will happen to you, too, if you fail when it's your turn. I didn't want to tell you before, but maybe now you know it will be an extra incentive to you.'

I start to watch what's happening with greatly renewed interest. Quisic has slipped his robe off now and is walking round, quite uninhibitedly, with the most enormous hard-on. It's strange to be spying on this room full of men and being able to see how differently they behave when they think no women are present.

Quisic takes the brush from the bowl and coats his penis

The Pleasure Ring

with the syrup from tip to base. Almost immediately I see him start to grow even longer and larger.

The equipment he's going to use is there ready for him. It's well worn and I can't help wondering how many other women over the years have been pleasured to unconsciousness on that mat and then entered without knowing it. From one wall he unhooks two woven straps attached to a rope. The rope rises up to a ring high in the ceiling above him and then back down to another fixing on the wall. Keeping the Irish girl lying on her front, he slips the straps over each of her ankles and then quickly pulls on the other end of the rope so that her feet are pulled up into the air, raised almost level with his waist.

He ties off the rope there, leaving her suspended only on her breasts and elbows. Ladisa whispers to me that this is the classic Arabic lovemaking position, the Courtesan's Bow. In this position the female is held curved back in such a way that even the most visited or over-orgasmed of vaginas is stretched and tightened to make it as narrow as that of a young virgin. Quisic straddles himself over the back of her raised legs, just behind her buttocks. Then, squatting down onto her, he pushes his penis forwards and downwards between her inner thighs to make a passage up into her. His tip enters her sex easily but, even though he's well lubricated, I can see full entry is as difficult as it's meant to be. He has to open her up with short, stabbing strokes, going in just a little deeper each time until he's buried up to the hilt.

He braces himself over her and for a long time he can only stand to move in and out of her tightness a tiny amount. I hear his breathing getting more ragged as each demanding thrust takes him closer to orgasm. Still in another world, the girl smiles happily to herself as Quisic uses her to inch himself to the final stages of arousal.

Only when the moment is upon him is he able to endure the sensation of pushing right in and out of her. Four knee-trembling strokes take him to the point of no return.

His hand gropes for the silk cord lying between her buttock cheeks. At the very second of ejaculation he pulls it sharply, jolting the first bead out of her. He makes her jerk involuntarily, contracting so hard round his shaft that it's plain it chokes off the flow of his come completely.

He's jetting unstoppably now, but he tortures himself by tugging the beads out of her anus slowly, one after the other, so that she stays in constant, unyielding spasm round him. I can almost feel him pumping blind against the vice-like grip of her sex, building up pressure inside himself. It's obviously a matter of pride how long he can stand it, how slowly he can pull the cord.

Muscles are standing out all over Quisic's straining body now, veins pulsing, eyes rolling. Finally, he has to retrieve the last bead. As it slips out of her, she relaxes open and immediately he fires all of his pent-up come into her in one long, cock-bursting jet that makes him cry out in exquisite pain.

The force of his single, great spurt of spunk lifts the Irish girl's whole body forward. The men in the crowd cheer in admiration, but I turn away, more determined than ever before that this will not become my fate.

Chapter 26

It's the night after this that finds me lying in my bed, touching the pleasure ring and thinking of all that has happened before.

I have little doubt that the second Dutch whore will be nearing the end of her Ordeal soon and I picture the state Quisic will have driven her to by now. I can only hope that at the same time tomorrow night I will still be reaching climaxes.

My greatest advantage is that I'm going to be allowed to wear the pleasure ring. Ladisa has consulted with Quisic and he has pronounced that there is nothing laid down in the rules of the competition that forbids the wearing of such devices.

I tell myself that, with all the extra stimulation I feel with the ring holding out my clitoris, Quisic is bound to be able to bring me to more orgasms than anyone else, including Angel.

As I drift off to sleep, I try to hold that reassuring thought in my mind.

Sometime in the darkest hours of the night, I'm disturbed by the faint creaking of the doorlatch being eased open. Before I can muster my wits, four burly men burst into the room and pin me down on the bed. I'm gagged immediately. I struggle bravely, but it's useless, they're too strong for me.

I have no idea who these men are. They're all swathed in grey, flowing desert robes, their features masked by a wrapping from their turbanned headdresses pulled down across their faces. But, when a fifth person enters the room, even though they're disguised the same way, I know who it is straight away.

Angel!

She spits out orders to the men. 'Bring her quickly! But be very careful, don't mark her in any way!'

Despite her veil I can still sense her gloating delight at capturing me. As I'm bundled into a set of the grey robes and dragged towards the door she turns to speak to someone else outside the room.

'We have her. Now take us to this hidden place of yours!'

I can hardly believe it when I see the person she's talking to is Ladisa.

My heart sinks to realise that the one friend I thought I had in Pernia, the one person I really believed I could trust, has betrayed me. All this time she's been on Angel's side, working for her, spying on me and reporting back everything I've said and done.

And how well she's done her job. I remember now the clever way she persuaded me not to go to the Prince and tell him of my treatment at Angel's hands. If something happens to me tonight no one will know anything of our past meetings and her mistress will be free of suspicion.

One glance would be enough to let Ladisa see exactly what I think of her now, but she studiously avoids looking in my direction and goes on ahead.

She seems to know every inch of the Palace. For the

The Pleasure Ring

second night running I'm guided by her, unobserved, through its shadowy back alleys. But how very different the circumstances of our journey are tonight! This time I'm being pulled along, held tightly by her hired thugs as they hurry after her.

After many winding twists and turns, we arrive at some long-forgotten doorway in the outer wall. She has a key for the stiff lock, but it takes one of her men to force the door far enough open on its rusty hinges for us to pass through.

I'm pushed through a tangle of overgrown bushes to find we've emerged at the most distant point of the Palace from the city. To the left of us, sand dunes stretch away to the starry horizon. In front of us stand olive groves. But, to our right, lies the royal burial grounds.

Here the barren landscape has been transformed into a range of bare hills, each surmounted by imposing marble tombs and mausoleums. It's towards these mounds that Ladisa leads us.

Once we've descended into the rocky valleys between the hills, we're entirely hidden from sight of the Palace. There's an eerie chill to this place – it's no wonder there's no one else around.

When we come to one of the largest tomb buildings, Ladisa turns and starts climbing. But she doesn't take the marked track. She makes off at an angle from it and halfway up she suddenly veers off and disappears from view through a hidden cleft in the rocks.

I'm made to follow her through the gap and into the passageway that lies beyond, worming its way into the centre of the hill, right to the very heart of the underground vaults.

At the very end, it opens out into a long corridor that

connects all the basement antechambers to the main tomb room. Faint moonlight filters in through gratings in the ceiling. When I look up I can see the night sky through the great glass dome of the mausoleum high above.

Angel orders lamps to be lit and turns to address me approvingly. 'What an excellent place this is going to be for us to conduct our business together, Amande. Hardly anyone ever comes near here, even during the daytime. Not that it would matter anyway. The walls are feet thick. No one will hear your cries.'

She sees the look of fear on my face. 'Oh yes! I'm afraid there is going to be a little pain involved in what has to be done. Still that can't be helped!'

I start to struggle again and she quickly motions for the men to take me into one of the rooms that open off from the corridor.

There's a slab-like table in the middle of the floor. My robe and gag are taken from me and I'm laid back lengthways over the table top with my hips balanced on the edge and my legs hanging down to the ground.

I'm restrained in the simplest, but cruellest, of ways. A latticed metal screen with a hooped archway cut out of it is placed over my waist. The men fix it down firmly so that it stands upright across the edge of the table with the arch fitted close round my belly. I'm free to move every part of me, but the hoop fits so tight I can neither slide upwards nor downwards out of it. I can thrash about as wildly as I like, but I'm completely trapped.

Even worse, I can see the lower part of my body through the screen, but I can't get my hands through it to prevent Angel doing what she likes to me.

She comes to stand just out of kicking range, smiling down at me.

The Pleasure Ring

'I believe you've already met the man that loaned this building to Ladisa for the night. His name's Kalim. Does that ring a bell? Perhaps you can recollect the purpose he keeps this secret hideaway for? It was when Ladisa told me of the depravities that he carries out here that I first conceived my plan to spoil your chances of winning the Ordeal. Kalim couldn't have been more helpful, he's supplied everything I need.'

She crosses over to a wooden cabinet standing against the wall and opens it to take out a huge brass syringe. She speaks sharply to two of the men and they spring forward to grasp one of my ankles each. They hoist my legs right up into the air and then split them wide, exposing both openings between my legs to her.

Angel tauntingly trails her fingers down over the folds of my labia, pausing thoughtfully as she encounters the glinting gold of the pleasure ring.

Then she takes the syringe in both hands and forces the long nozzle of it past the tight rosebud of my anus and into the tunnel beyond. Ignoring my pleas, she squeezes the plunger in slowly and empties the contents of the barrel deep inside me. I feel the cold, jelly-like stickiness of the oily lubricant coursing far up into my back passage.

Now she returns to the cabinet and brings out a sickening object – a thick, balloon-shaped bladder attached to a pair of bellows by a long pipe.

'I see you've already guessed what this clever little tool is for. It is Kalim's instrument for preparing his way before he takes his special pleasure with his young "virgin" boys. Of course, he only uses it to ease his entry, but I intend to take things much farther!

'I'm going to put the bladder up inside you and inflate it so hard that it will stretch you beyond recovery.

'You'll be taken back to the Palace just in time for your Ordeal tomorrow night. Quisic will try to stimulate you on the *hi-jin*, but, mysteriously, any attempt at sexual contraction will cause you so much pain you'll be totally unable to reach orgasm. Your complete failure will be a great disappointment to everyone. You'll be disgraced, but the best part is, even if you try and blame me, there will be no proof. No evidence at all except for a little redness inside your arse. It's a perfect plan, don't you think? Let me show you the start of it now.'

She begins to feed the gathered end of the deflated bladder into my slippery opening. It's not put all the way in, only halfway so that the fullest part of the bladder will be pressing against the ring of my anus when it's blown up.

As soon as it's in place she signals to the two men to let my feet drop down to the floor once more. I struggle into a sitting position, trying to reach over the top of the screen and tear the vile thing out of me. But there's no way I can reach past it. It's so maddening!

'Prepare yourself, Amande!'

She starts to pump the bellows and I feel the bladder swelling. Soon it's distending me uncomfortably. I can't bear to sit up anymore. I lay back flat on the table, moaning out with the feeling inside me.

She works at the bellows steadily. There's no pain yet, but I know I'm being opened up a long way. It feels nasty, makes me have to breathe really deeply.

The outer end of the bladder is expanding too. Bulging out humiliatingly between my cheeks, spreading them right apart. As she carries on, the enormous swelling balloon pillows my thighs up higher and higher, until, finally, my toes are lifted off the floor and my legs become

The Pleasure Ring

supported by the bladder, their weight just adding to the forces pressing inside me.

Angel searches my face for the first sign of distress. And when it comes I see her eyes shining. She drops the bellows and hurries excitedly to the top end of the table. She cups my head and lifts it up to let me look down the length of my body. I groan when I see what she's done to me. My hips are thrust upwards unnaturally, my belly drawn in tight, my thighs and legs parted and hanging in mid-air. My vulva is distorted from below in a way that's pushed my clitoris out of me like a nipple. I can feel it straining inside the pleasure ring, its domed peak the highest point on my whole body.

Angel comes closer and whispers in my ear, 'Look at the men! Look what you're making them do!'

They're trying to hide it, but I can tell the four men are touching themselves under their robes as they lean back against the wall, watching everything. Even from here I can see their robes moving as they furtively stroke their erections. I'm just surprised Ladisa isn't with them. I would have thought she, of all people, would have wanted to see this.

'There's no reason for us to hurry this, Amande. Why don't we give them something to really get excited about? Why don't we let them see me making you come?'

I snarl at her, wrenching my head away from her hands. How could she imagine I would ever orgasm for her, no matter how hard she tries to make me?

Undeterred, she returns to the other side of the screen. She drains a few last drops of lubricant from the syringe over her fingertips and I grit my teeth as she begins to stroke them over the red slash of my hairless mound.

I can ignore what she's doing until she delves two fingers

into my sex. She starts to frig them into me like a cock and it makes me gasp out. How can that feel so good?

I hate myself for even thinking like this. But it's been so very, very long since I last came.

Her other hand curves underneath me to grasp the grotesque bulge of the bladder in her palm. She starts to squeeze it rhythmically, pulsing my legs up and down, throbbing the hidden end so far inside me it makes me feel queasy.

Now her lips are on the very nub of my clitoris, teasing it where it blossoms out of the ring. I've been tightened and tightened, coiled like a spring in preparation for that massive release tomorrow. And now it's so hard not to let just a little of all that pent-up tension spill out of me.

Sensing my weakening, her tongue goes faster, her fingers harder. I don't know what to do to stop her exciting me like this. I'm still tender from Ladisa's beating, but that's not enough.

I could control myself if it wasn't for the bladder, wasn't for the way she's using it on me. She's massaging my anus so strongly that I keep thinking that, somehow, she's 'masturbating' it.

I begin to hammer my fists on the table in a passion of anger and want. Angel tears her head away from me. 'I know you're going to come. I can taste it!'

I shout back, 'You bitch, Angel! You bloody bitch!' but I can't deny what she's saying. I can't hold myself back now. I just need to come so badly.

It's wonderful to feel the aching glow gathering inside me again after all these weeks. I'm lost now, beyond saving. Despite everything, I start to orgasm.

But it's so different from normal. So much farther back.

The Pleasure Ring

And I suddenly realise it's like that because it's not my clitoris that's causing it.

I call out. 'Noooo-oh, no! Not this!'

I can't believe what's happening, but it's true.

I'm coming from behind!

Angel is actually making me climax inside my anus!

When it's finally finished she stands up, wiping my wetness from her lips in triumph.

'You never could say no, could you, Amande? Not in Paris, not in that brothel in Angers. Not even here, like this, you little slut! I only hope you enjoyed it – because it's going to be the last for a long time!'

She turns to the four men.

'You've seen enough! Leave us now. The rest of this is between me and her. Bring yourselves off outside while you wait. That is if you haven't done so already!'

For some strange reason the men don't obey her this time. The three others look over at their leader and, when he makes no move, they stand firm as well.

Angel points to the door with an angry finger. 'Didn't you hear what I said? Get out! Go away!'

The leader begins to calmly unwind his scarf. As he loosens it, he says to Angel sternly, 'That's enough, El-Marrach. Hold your tongue!'

She starts to retort, 'How dare you speak to . . .' but the rest of her sharp words die away unspoken. For at that moment the mask falls away and the angry face of Prince Hassan is revealed to us both!

Angel makes a sudden dash for the door, but his men block her flight.

'I'm sorry, my dear, there will be no escape. On this occasion, it is you that has been deceived. All the time you thought Ladisa was working for you she was really acting on my orders. When she told me what you had planned for tonight I knew I had to see for myself just how wicked you could really be.

'I've had you under watch for quite a while and I haven't liked any of what I've learnt. This affair with Amande is the final straw, but you can be assured I am going to make you pay for all your wrongdoings.'

He orders his men to take her away, then he calls Ladisa in and discreetly leaves her to release me from my embarrassing restraints.

The second we're alone we both fall over ourselves to be the first to apologise. Ladisa for tricking me into thinking she's betrayed me, me for believing she ever would. Happily, by the time I'm free we're completely reconciled.

She drapes my robes back round me again and escorts me to the door. Prince Hassan is waiting there, anxious to speak with me. He takes me to one side and stands awkwardly in front of me.

'Amande, can you ever forgive me for putting you through that? You must know I would never have let El-Marrach hurt you. I never intended things to go that far. But when she began to do those things to you I was so aroused I couldn't help myself. I know I should have stopped her, but the temptation of watching her making you come was too great to resist. And now I'm ashamed of myself and you must think very badly of me.'

He seems so sorry, I really can't be cross with him. My eyes meet his and something that surprises us both passes between us. He lays his hands on my shoulders and draws me near to him. I'm sure he would have kissed me then if one of his men hadn't chosen that moment to approach and deliver his report.

The Pleasure Ring

Hassan releases me reluctantly. 'Come, Amande. We will leave this place soon, but first I have something for you.'

He shows me into another of the small chambers. Like the first, Kalim has pressed it into use for his sex sessions. There is no table in this room though, only two pillars that support the floor above. They divide the room in two and stand just more than an arm's span apart.

Angel is there in the room too. Stripped and chained by hands and feet, stretched out between the two pillars in a taut X shape.

She's facing away from us, but she doesn't try to turn when she hears us enter. I notice that she can hardly keep still. Her hips are squirming backwards and forwards, her head languishing to one side, her sex swollen open and brazenly wet.

One whole wall of the chamber is covered with shelves of deviant sexual devices. There are whips and riding crops, sets of tapered anal dildoes in ever-increasing sizes, enormous studded phalluses, mechanical dilators, masturbation sleeves, even a disgusting machine: a wooden frame holding a long, cock-shaped shaft that slides in and out at buttock height. The shaft is connected by belts and levers to a pedal on the floor. It's plain the frame's designed so that Kalim can stand it behind him and work the pedal with his foot to penetrate himself from the rear at the same time as he enters his restrained victims.

The Prince speaks to me in a loud voice, wanting Angel to hear what he's saying as well. 'Now is your chance to take your revenge, Amande. Do what you want with her, she's absolutely at your mercy!'

I let my eyes rove over the huge choice before me,

allowing myself to imagine all the terrible things I could do to Angel with the implements Kalim has collected here.

I step over to the whips to examine them more closely and I hear her whimper.

But it's almost a cry of ecstatic anticipation. Her thighs are quivering with nothing less than ill-disguised expectation.

She wants this! She's almost coming off with the thought of being punished mercilessly by me in some obscene way.

It's that cry that makes my decision. I slip my hands down inside my robe and deftly unclip the pleasure ring from between my legs. Walking round the room, I look her straight in the eye.

'Now *you* are in my power. But, if I was to hurt you in any way, it would make me as bad as you. And I have no wish to sink that low.

'So I'm not going to do anything more than return your gift. From the first day you gave me the pleasure ring, it has brought me nothing but bad luck. I only hope it will not do the same for you now it is yours.

'I wish you no harm, Angel, but take care that our paths do not cross again. Next time I may not be so forgiving.'

With that I reach down and gently part her labia. Her clitoris is very big. It lolls out of her like a tiny, engorged tongue. I smack it sharply to bring it to full attention and then I snap the gold ring tight round it as far back as it will go.

She starts to shout at me now. Goading and taunting me, trying to provoke me to such anger that I snatch down a whip from the wall and flay her high-cheeked buttocks with it. She longs for me to inflict the savage,

The Pleasure Ring

stinging pain, craves the frenzied orgasm she knows it will bring her to.

And I know my cruellest punishment is to deny her.

So I simply turn and walk away.

Chapter 27

Hassan has arranged carriages to take us all back to the Palace. I'm glad I don't have to walk because I feel completely drained now.

For a reason I'm too tired to ask about, I'm taken to new apartments right in the very heart of the Palace. Ladisa helps me into the bed and I fall asleep so quickly I don't even remember her leaving the room.

It's late afternoon before I wake again, roused by the bedroom being flooded in sunshine as the shutters are flung open.

Half blinded by the light I make out the figure of Prince Hassan standing by the window. He gestures to me to come and join him. My robes have been taken away so I modestly gather a bedsheet round myself as I go to stand beside him.

I find I'm looking down into a square that opens onto one of the main courtyards. Below us, some of Hassan's soldiers are preparing a fine horse ready for a journey. As I watch its rider is brought out and placed on it.

It is Angel, tightly bound and still unclothed. The ropes that hold her crisscross over her chest, separating and pushing out her two full breasts. The soldiers lift her sideways over the saddle, head on one side, feet on the other. They tie her across it like that, with her bottom thrust up into the air. An officer approaches her now. He has the brass syringe that Angel used on me last night. Probing the nozzle between her buttocks, he finds her sex and fills it with oil.

A soldier arrives holding one of the largest dildoes from Kalim's collection. Even from here it looks enormous, the soldier has to carry it in both hands to support it. The officer takes it and presses it into Angel wetly, twisting it back and forth to work it right into her.

There is a little leather loop on the end of the phallus. The captain threads a leather belt through it and then passes it under her belly and round her thighs. When he buckles it tight I see Angel's head strain back as even more of the gross shaft is forced up inside her.

Hassan takes my hand. 'You may have been able to spare El-Marrach, but I could not. It is necessary that she is punished and seen to be punished.

'She will be paraded through the streets like this for everyone to see and then she will be sent on her way from the city gates at sunset. The horse knows its way home, but the journey ahead of El-Marrach will be a long and unpleasant one.'

I can't help thinking, privately, of how the heaviness of the dildo will weight Angel's sex down onto the saddle, make her ringed clitoris chafe unceasingly against the worn leather. It will indeed be a very long journey for her! I wonder how many times the vigorous rubbing will force her to 'arrive' herself before the horse reaches its destination.

'The stallion you see belongs to my cousin, Prince Youssef. I am returning it to him, sending El-Marrach with it as a special gift. Youssef is ruler of one of my cities on the far side of the desert. He is famous throughout the land for having the largest penis in all Pernia. El-Marrach's

The Pleasure Ring

unusual saddling will ensure that by the time she reaches him she will have been readied many times over for the welcome he will give her. I am sure he will pleasure himself with her freely for a while. But then he will put her to a very different use.

'Youssef has some very bizarre ideas. He firmly believes his member has grown to the size it is because every morning he dips it into a bowl filled with the dewy liquor collected from the climaxed vulvas of his harem of slave women. He keeps a dozen or so women just for that purpose, all looked after by eunuchs.

'Each day before dawn, the women are taken to a room and tethered on all fours in a row, like so many cows or goats. The eunuchs move up and down the line behind them, masturbating the women to climax with their fingers. But at the same time they insert special wooden probes into their vaginas, skilfully stimulating certain hidden places and causing their lubrication to flow uncontrollably.

'As soon as they orgasm, their vulvas are milked vigorously and the precious wetness is expelled into narrow silver dishes pushed up between their thighs. The eunuchs are ruthless, climaxing the women again and again without pity so that the bowl can be filled quickly and taken to Youssef whilst it is still warm.

'Before too long El-Marrach will take her own place amongst these women. For one so licentious as her it will be an especially harsh punishment. The act that was her greatest pleasure will soon become her greatest bane. By the time Youssef has finished with her I doubt if she will ever want to come again!'

Hassan's voice changes now, becomes more serious. 'I do have other news for you as well, Amande. I have to tell you I have decided to cancel the Ordeal. You will be glad to hear that it will not now be necessary for you to attempt to become my new concubine.'

I feel tears suddenly welling up in my eyes. I see all my dreams, all my secret hopes of happiness, crumbling away. Hassan hurries to continue.

'Hear me out first. This year was to be the last competition anyway. I have long thought that it is time I took a wife and gave up my old ways. El-Marrach knew this and that was why she was so desperate to win again this year and secure her position.

'When we were in the tomb chambers last night, I offered you the chance to take your revenge on her, but you refused. Not one in a hundred women would have acted with the grace and dignity that you showed. It was at that moment that I knew in my head what my heart has been telling me ever since the first time I saw you.

'Amande, I love you and I want you to become my wife.'

He puts his fingers to my lips. 'No, you don't have to answer now. It is the tradition in Pernia that couples such as you and I spend a period of time together first to discover if we are truly suited. For the moment it is only necessary that you tell me you are willing to become engaged to me for the next three months. Only then will I ask you again formally if you wish to marry me.'

His eyes fall to the floor with that streak of shyness I find so attractive. 'There is one aspect of this engagement that you should be aware of, though. Our laws do state that the three months are strictly a time for the strengthening of friendship and affection. From the moment of the announcement, sexual contact of any kind is absolutely forbidden and forcibly prohibited. It is demanded that both our sex parts are restrained in such

The Pleasure Ring

a way that orgasmic release is made impossible. Come, let me show you.'

Leading me away from the window, he quietly pulls open the front of his robe. Underneath, his genitals are closely cupped in a tiny silk pouch. He releases the ties and his already stiffening cock unfurls to full hardness.

He takes my hand and, self-consciously, folds my fingers round the base of his shaft. He whispers hoarsely for me to pull his foreskin fully forward and shudders with emotion when I do as he bids.

'Look here! See at the end. See where I've been pierced already.'

He points out a circle of tiny holes ringed all around the fold of loose skin.

'This was done when I had to be forced to abstain for the month before my Coming of Age ceremony. These holes will be used again this time. A silver wire will be passed through them and my foreskin will be gathered closed so that I am unable to pull it back and expose the sensitive head beneath.'

Aroused with lust now, I slowly let my sheet drop to the floor and stand before him, naked.

'You must show me where I will be restricted!'

His shaking fingers stray to my breasts. 'The woman's nipples are thought to be dangerously sensitive. Gold caps will be fitted over the whole teat to prevent all stimulation. Each will be held in place by a pin that passes right through the cap, spearing the nipple inside.'

His hands slide downwards over my belly and dip between my thighs. I part my legs with a sigh. He starts to kiss hungrily at my neck as he speaks now. 'The sex, of course, must also be attended to. Both of your outer lips will be pierced in seven places. Tiny gold padlocks will be passed through each pair of holes, drawing the labia tightly closed and guarding the treasures inside.

'But that is not the end of it, for it is also written that virtuousness can only truly be proved when it is tested!

'When the wire has been inserted round the tip of my member, a long chain will be secured to it and a brass ball attached to the other end. The chain will hang down to the floor between my legs so that, wherever I go, the ball will trail behind me, dragging and catching on the ground. My foreskin will be continually jerked and twisted, teasing my cockhead from morning to night.'

We're entwined together now. His fingers are exploring my sex, caressing my tingling clitoris. My own hands begin to massage his erection, now standing fiery hot.

'What will they do to me, Hassan!'

'The testing of the female is more subtle. Firstly, bangles will be forged round your ankles and each of the seven locks through your labia will be linked to a single ring by gold chains. Then two more chains will be used to join the bangles to the single ring.

'But the chains will deliberately be made short, measured just so long that when you step forward each pulls tight and gently plucks at the labia. You will find that the act of walking will cause your vulva to be tugged from side to side, endlessly massaged in the most disturbing way. I'm told climbing stairs becomes quite breathtaking!

'It will never be enough to bring release, though. Only sufficient to keep you in a constant state of agitated frustration. By the time our engagement is over we will both be unbelievably excited for each other.'

I gasp into his ear, 'I will do anything you ask, but don't you realise how difficult it will be for me. I've already denied myself for the past six weeks, preparing for the

The Pleasure Ring

Ordeal. You saw last night what that's done to me, how close I am to coming all the time. I can't endure another three months of abstinence. I can't do without you for all that time. I need you now!'

Hassan begins to press me down onto the bed. 'Perhaps it would be better if we postponed the announcement until tonight. To give me time to relieve your suffering.'

I fall back sensuously against the pillows, writhing with want. 'Do you think that will be long enough. It has been such a long time. Maybe tomorrow morning would be better.'

He groans. 'Amande, my darling, from the look on your face now, I see it could take me until tomorrow night to satisfy you completely! Let me start my task straight away!'

And with that he slides himself between my thighs and I feel his beautiful cock entering me for the first of many times.